No
Holmes
Barred

Edited by Paul Thomas Miller

DEDICATION

Dedicated to all Sherlockians and Holmesians:
whichever game you play, however you play it,
play nicely and, most of all, enjoy yourself.

CONTENTS

ACKNOWLEDGMENTS

Many thanks to:

Arthur Conan Doyle, The Founder of the Feast,

Every one of our contributors

and Nicko Vaughan for
the moral support and massive help editing

Introduction

Readers choosing this first volume from Doyle's Rotary Coffin may be surprised to find it is not what one might think of as a normal Holmesian anthology. While it is a collection of works with a vague Holmesian theme running through it, it is more of a scrapbook - a collection of wildly varying contents: fiction, poetry, essays, and art celebrating Holmes in many ways, from the traditional to the most outré Holmeses imaginable.

The creative contributors vary wildly as well in their backgrounds, viewpoints, talents, experiences, and strengths. This collection celebrates the established successful authors and artists and those taking their first tentative steps into Holmesian creativity. That is the point – to celebrate all these works in their varying styles and strengths as no interpretation of Holmes is wrong. Doyle's Rotary Coffin firmly believes any attempt at interpreting Holmes has value.

When Doyle's Rotary Coffin first nebulously formed in internet discussions, it was all about celebrating every iteration of Holmes, regardless of whether we individually agree with any specific iteration, or even actually like whatever form it may take. The ethos of the society can be summed up by its motto – No Holmes Barred. Whatever your conception of Holmes is and however you enjoy it, we love it for you and celebrate it for you. We love your enthusiasm, your desire to bring it to life and your contribution to the ever-changing and yet never-changing face of Sherlock Holmes.

All Holmesians have their own idea of Holmes. They are all different: Gay, straight, autistic, psychotic, bi-polar, Victorian, contemporary, male, female, human, animal, alien, robot and anything else. One of the fascinating things about Holmes is that whenever he is written about by a Holmesian, they can twist him and his universe in any way they desire but he will always remain recognisable. There are some solid twisted examples included here. You may enjoy them, or not. Hopefully you will enjoy the energy behind them, and perhaps even meet a new friend along the way. Holmesiana brings together people from so many different walks of life. Holmes is such a strong character that he can build bridges between people instantly.

All this variety gives us one of the supreme joys of Holmesiana: seeing Holmes through other people's eyes. When people share what they love about Holmes, their insights or the way they play with the character, we are invited to view the Canon all over again. Those sixty stories get to be fresh and exciting once again, by proxy.

Doyle's Rotary Coffin is an all-inclusive society. If you would like to become a member, you already are. If you'd like to seal the deal, you can print yourself off a membership card from the website – doylesrotarycoffin.com – but you don't have to. Since you are here, with this volume in your hands, we hope you accept our invitation to share the Holmesian enthusiasm of others in ways you may not have considered otherwise.

No Holmes barred!

Paul Thomas Miller

It Is No Easy Task
By Margie Deck

Speaking of incidents in the life of Sherlock Holmes, Sir Arthur recalled Mr. Gillette's preparation for the presentation of the famous detective on the stage. 'Mr. Gillette,' he said, 'wired to me from America asking if he might marry Sherlock Holmes in the play. I replied at once, "Marry him, kill him, or do what you like with him!"

Daily Mail (8 October 1904, p. 3)

Sir Arthur Conan Doyle
Incorporeal Spirit, Location Unknown
American Exchange, Strand — to be left till called for

My dear Sir,

It is with perhaps a touch of hubris that I attempt to speak to you at this late date, but I'm afraid I must do so, as the situation is becoming an impossible one. The flood-gate you opened with your rashly given permission to Mr. Gillette, and thereafter appropriated by thousands upon thousands, concerning Holmes — 'Marry him, kill him, or do what you like with him!' — has left me seriously inconvenienced by you. How is a faithful reader to remain above water in such a deluge? And further, how does one create his own unique contribution to such a collection? Surely almost any effort will lack distinction, as a drop of water must inevitably become indistinguishable from any other drop in an Atlantic or a Niagara. I confess the situation leaves an unpleasant effect upon my mind.

As you noted as long ago as 1926, 'the public has lost the sense of novelty with Holmes and his methods. This has been helped by the repeated Parodies.' Indeed. I must note that your permissive attitude towards adaptation certainly has not helped the situation. I grant that this permissiveness with the Holmes stories is not so surprising considering your admission, 'I have never taken them seriously myself.' Perhaps you should have taken the adaptation matter more seriously.

Let us consider the first part of your flippant direction,

'Marry him.' Here, you give permission to degrade a series of logic-driven adventures into a course of tales forever tinged with romanticism. Well, Sir, I should not offend your intelligence by explaining what is obvious, but you allowed for a man who 'never loved' to be contorted into every possible type of romantic entanglement. Actually, a few of them may only be possible on the written page, as some laws of physics do matter.

I will omit the onerous details, but even with all my omissions, there is enough to startle and amaze. No doubt there exists a tale of romance between Holmes and an injured lady, a cannibal, a wooden-legged ruffian, a conventional dragon, a wicked earl, and any other horror the human mind can imagine. The desire to combine Holmes and romance stimulates the imagination. As you may remember: where there is no imagination, there is no horror. Could you possibly have foreseen the horrific results of this part of your response to Mr. Gillette? Unfortunately, that ship has sailed, leaving the faithful reader and aspiring contributor further incommoded.

The unhealthy excitement continues with the second part of your directive: 'kill him.' Apparently, there is still nothing new under the sun. Your original work included a death for Holmes, and yet you gave permission for it to be done again. And it has been done, and done, and done until your faithful reader despairs of any hope of originality or mystery. Occasionally an author has surrounded the death with outré and sensational accompaniments, but it is a mistake to confound strangeness with mystery. No new or special features can be drawn from what is now a commonplace little murder, and I find myself absolutely hampered in my plans.

When a doctor does go wrong, he is the first of criminals, and you, Sir, despite your nerve and knowledge, went terribly wrong with the final part of your instruction to Mr. Gillette: 'do what you like with him!' Could you not anticipate and prevent the inevitable torrent of public participation? What do the public, the great unobservant public, care about the finer shades of analysis and deduction?

Instead, one is subjected to every imaginable contortion of

Holmes and his world. An enormous multitude of individuals took it upon themselves to create their own alternative — each grotesquely improbable, no doubt, but still just conceivable. Were you perhaps encouraged by the judicious stimulation of large cheques sent to you by devious methods? You might be startled to learn that the Holmes world has become so twisted as to have Dr. Watson competently solving cases. Yes, Watson! And this despite your own insistence that 'Watson never for one instant as chorus and chronicler transcends his own limitations.' Not limiting itself to twisting Watson, this public also has Lestrade competently solving cases, as well as the housekeeper, the other Holmes brother, various previous clients, and assorted street urchins. I have never read such rubbish in my life.

The enthusiasm for creating such ineffable twaddle continues unabated. Any attempt at a critical review of this inundation is bound to be lost in the tremendous abyss. So much public attention has now been drawn to the subject of Sherlock Holmes that no good purpose can be served by affecting to disregard what is a common subject for conversation. Therefore now, at the close of April, I find myself placed in such a position through your careless persecution that I am in positive danger of losing my liberty to create original extensions or critical exegeses.

Oh, it drives me half-mad to think of, and I cannot sleep a wink at night. I often resort to a large correspondence, twenty or thirty a day, 280 characters at a time, to discuss the matter with others, although no two of them write exactly alike. The correspondents often have a way of wandering into unlikely positions (there are always some lunatics about — it would be a dull world without them), and then I begin to give myself virtuous airs. What could be more hopelessly prosaic and immaterial?

What then is left? I see no possible solution beyond the laying aside any creative aspirations and returning to simply rereading the sixty-some oddly original tales you created. I don't think anyone could make much of this choice, but if they should, I will tell them: 'You work your own method, and I shall work mine.'

Perhaps you see nothing remarkable in my decision to

limit myself to only reading your original Sherlock Holmes work on account of your permissive liberality. But wait a moment! Was this a subtle trap, a clever forecast of coming events? (You have all the cleverness which makes a successful man.) Were you looking far into the future? This is a trick that you are playing upon me. He he! You are a funny one. Never mind me. I shall stand behind a holly bush and see what I can see.

Pray give my greetings to Mrs. Doyle, and believe me to be, my dear fellow,

Very sincerely yours,

A. Prolix Riposte

Giant Tentacle Holmes by Spacefall

The Importance of Silly Holmes
By Mattias Boström

I am an Embracer. I find most Sherlock Holmes related things interesting. They are all part of the Sherlockian universe – books, films, stuff, good, bad, funny, boring.

I think you can pretty much do whatever you want with Sherlock Holmes and Dr. Watson. You can't expect everyone to like it, but you are fully entitled to do it. And I will especially appreciate every attempt to do something unexpected, a new perspective, congenial or not. I already have the originals, now I want something else, something that will wake me up – no matter if I like it or not. Because if you do take the risks and invest your intelligence and time in trying to do clever things with something that is so close to my heart, you will get my embrace. The opposite – which is if you don't do anything at all – is a much more boring alternative. So, come on, shake up Sherlock, and I will give you my love.

On numerous occasions in 2019, I discussed and defended the film Holmes & Watson (with Will Ferrell and John C. Reilly). You may wonder why, since it is just a silly film about Sherlock Holmes. My main concern is not to say that this is a good film, because even if I liked it, I'm fully aware that I belong to a minority of the viewers. No, my main concern is to defend its right to exist – and to tell you why we need even more Sherlock Holmes silliness.

When Sherlock Holmes was more of a recent success, back in the 1890s, what made Holmes popular was not just Conan Doyle's original stories, but there was also another Holmes – a parallel Holmes – which developed mainly thanks to all the parodies. And that Holmes, often a quite silly Holmes and always disguised under a parody name, became as popular as the original Holmes. Soon there were more stories about silly Holmes than original stories by Conan Doyle. I would like to go as far as saying that without silly Holmes there wouldn't have been the popular culture icon Holmes. Silly parallel Holmes was a set of Holmes characteristics dressed up as stories. Nowadays, silly Holmes is seldom used for stories, but he turns up in the most unexpected ways – in advertising, children's books, jokes, as a funny disguise in TV episodes, etc. Original Holmes and more serious adaptations are of course essential for the popular culture status of Sherlock Holmes, but it is through the parallel – and often quite silly – Holmes that people outside the Sherlockian world are constantly reminded about a detective in deerstalker with a pipe and a magnifying glass, sometimes called Sherlock Holmes, and sometimes called nothing at all, because he needs no introduction.

Weird adaptations and curious uses of Sherlock Holmes will never destroy the original stories. It will never diminish Sherlock Holmes's popularity. If that was the case, it would have happened a long time ago, in the 1890s. It's not even a question of quality, because the constant use of Sherlock Holmes is in itself what proves his popularity, not the popularity of every single adaptation.

We all have a right to have different views of adaptations, and to express those views. But when it comes to spreading rumors that in the end will destroy the chances for an adaptation to actually reach those who would enjoy being entertained by it, I think we need to remember that if we take away that other Sherlock Holmes – the silly, parallel one – we may soon lose the popularity of the original Sherlock Holmes, because they have always been dependent on each other.

This Fall on the HW
By Wanda and Jeff Dow

Eustace! James Garner stars as Eustace Brackenstall, a saucy septuagenarian used to getting his own way. But when he loses his money, he is forced to turn his home into a boarding house. The laughs ensue when Lady Brackenstall's (Carol Burnett) old boyfriend Crocker (Patrick Stewart) rents a room. From the creators of *My Mother the Car.* Thursdays at 8:00 PM.

The Art of Decoration. The great Austrian interior decorator brings his European ideas to America. Baron Gruner gives wonderful advice and hands-on tips for displaying anything and everything. In the premiere episode, he discusses Northern Wei dynasty pottery with Dr. Hill Barton. Saturdays at 9:00 AM.

Target Practice. Maria Pinto Gibson (Jennifer Lopez) is a police detective with a checkered past. When she teams up with partner Grace Dunbar (Jennifer Aniston) the laughs fly almost as fast as the ammo. From the producers of *Married ... With Children.* Tuesdays at 8:30 PM.

The Scowrers. A Film by Ken Burns. In this 78-hour epic, Ken Burns *(The Civil War, Brooklyn Bridge, Baseball)* details the rise and fall of this Gilmerton Mountain dynasty. Interviews with the descendants of Jack McGinty, James Scott, Ted Baldwin, and other Vermissa Valley residents. Wednesdays at 9:00 PM.

Secret Agent Man. Each week, master of disguise Neville St. Clair (Michael Richards) enters a world of beggars, crime, and decay. His job: do whatever he can to make the world safe. His only help: his wit and a jacket full of coins. From the producers of *Home Improvement.* Saturdays at 8:00 PM.

Eukenuba Presents The Grimpen Mire Dog Trials. Each week, the finest dogs from around the world compete to determine who is the fastest, most agile canine ever. In addition to the usual tunnel runs, levers, and jumps, the Grimpen Mire is famous for its Boulder Leaps, Marsh Swims, Mine Escapes and Phosphorescent Fur Paint competition. A challenge for both dog and owner. Thursdays at 7:30 PM.

Who Wants to Be an Ex-Millionaire? Host Charles August Milverton cajoles, threatens, and extorts his guests into giving up their money. Tuesdays and Fridays at 9:00 PM.

Churchscapes with Josiah. Josiah Amberley and his wife tour Europe painting the major churches in the capitals. The Amberleys show their inimitable techniques and reveal a secret or two in each episode. Saturdays at 10:00 AM.

Larry King of Bohemia Live. Moving from CNN, Larry King of Bohemia talks with the newsmakers of yesterday and today. Weekdays at 11:30 PM.

Brollylock Holmes
By Shai Porter

Chapter 1: Do Umbrellas Dream Of Electric Plugs?

Nothing. Not a single drop. And I'm about to go mad. I need some.

Eight days bundled tight in this constrictive strap, with an overwhelming desire for release.

It's no life for a Fox Model RGS2 Umbrella-- that's me by the way, hello--with a bespoke hollowed-out compartment concealed within the Malacca handle. The only one in the world. But am I out amongst the elements? No. I... am in a closet. It feels as if I have been in one for 128 years.

The wellies sit beside me-- placid, barely used-- as they are only worn when the act of walking through puddles is absolutely unavoidable. For our client, such legwork is a rarity. The mac, dusty with disuse. But I... I should be out there, whether amongst the deluge, with torrents out of control and nothing but my wiry frame and taut black fabric to protect him from the onslaught, or in a gentle mist, secure that I am there, should conditions ever worsen. This disuse is intolerable.

This is London, not Dubai. London– its streets a great cesspool into which all kinds of drifting, tumbling, airborne water is irresistibly drained. Eight days is far too long to have gone without any precipitation whatsoever, and a man of such regular habits would not abandon his sole means of protection. Therefore, there must be another--procured during my unfortunate and unavoidable absence, when I was detained at a security checkpoint in Eastern Europe for two weeks.

They hadn't appreciated my exceedingly sharp ferrule. Or rather... they had. Ever since the murder of Georgi Markov on the streets of London using a micro-engineered ricin pellet fired into the leg via an umbrella, security has been particularly cautious. Generally, airport employees miss my more... unique... features. They are idiots who lower the IQ of the whole continent. But this one, this particular worker, had been more observant than most. My client was forced to make the journey without me, returning to liberate me from that hellish prison only at the end of his appointment.

My replacement was likely another Fox, as no brand could possibly prove superior. Not enough time to make a custom handle. I deduce it is, therefore, a more elaborate one... trading my sleek practicality for a more decorative style. Bamboo, perhaps? Whatever it may be, we'll have to get rid of it. The trick is simply to be noticed again. He will remember my utility if I simply provide a reminder of what it was like...the thrill of the downpour, the water dripping over my ribs... just he and I against the forces of nature.

Of course, a plan will be required to escape this predicament, and being a high-functioning parapluie, any such plan would be easily conceived and actualised. Nearing twenty-to-eight. Precious little time, as he will soon be leaving the Diogenes for home. What have I to work with?

The fuse box is to my left, mid-way up the closet wall. A thick metal bar suspends the mac, a fur-trimmed winter coat, a three-piece suit, two impeccably starched collared shirts, and two ties. On the floor: dress shoes, wellies, snow boots. A large jug of bottled water which pains me to even so much as glance at, I so long to feel it beat against my canopy. It is bad enough sensing the heavy, humid air of this enclosed space against my springs. Next to it is a cardboard box, laden with several dense manuscripts. Above, a small silver protrusion-- a sprinkler system built into the ceiling-- and an equally small sensor vent in front. An access panel with what can only be a panic button-based alarm system lies far beyond my reach.

Even if I could somehow manage to trip it, it would not be enough if I merely called brief attention to myself as he as rushed past to disable the alarm-- doubtless thought triggered by a depleted battery. I need to be both seen and useful in order to be carried away in those graceful and competent hands once again. I rest my rib tips against my collar and think.

If the volume of material through which the current flows is smaller than the fusible link... Sparks...older copper wiring... files as combustibles...ignition temperatures to initiate a self-sustaining exothermic oxidation reaction. Of course, it could be dangerous, playing with fire, but he would come at once. What do I have access to which will catch easily enough, but won't produce flames strong enough to devour me? And can I produce a spark with which to coax it to life? Or, more to the point, can I produce smoke? Lots of it.

One occasionally nice thing about never living is you can never die... even if bits of you are jammed into a power outlet. It would damage my structure, of course, but not enough to impact functionality. And it would most certainly be painful. I can, indeed, feel. But it will be worth a wound--it will be worth many wounds-- to extricate myself from the depths of that closet and again know the loyalty and love which lay beyond it-- being held firmly in that cold mist once again.

Chapter 2: Rainy is the New Sexy

The dossier is packed tightly, creating almost a solid mass. With luck, it will be a slow burn. A quick tap to the mac and just a bit of dusty lint falls directly on me, making me feel that much drier. Wholly unpleasant. A few more blows, and I have a decent pile of highly flammable material, which I attempt to push around the area beneath the socket. I've only one chance. If it doesn't catch before the fuse blows, resetting the breaker would be theoretically possible, but far from guaranteed. I manage to balance a bit of the material on a rib tip and prepare myself as best I can for whatever impact making contact with the power source will have on my frame. I am not, myself, electric, but as a conductor of electricity, I am unbeatable.

It is painful. Pain is not a common thing in my experience. I try to analyse it, in the hopes that the distraction will make it more tolerable. It is of little help. No need to describe it to you. That benefits neither of us. But the end result is worth the effort. Starting with crackling and hissing, I will it to shut up and smoke. Then there are sparks. Many sparks. Beautiful, golden rain pours from the socket. The lint and dust on my rib has been dislodged, but the now melting tip, it is hot enough that a mere touch ignites the remaining mess at my ferrule. The papers smolder ever so slightly. I hope it is enough. When the smoke rises, the alarm will trigger, the sprinkler system will release, and I will be useful. Yes, an umbrella shouldn't be opened indoors, but neither should it ever be raining therein.

Now, I must achieve maximum visibility. I allow myself to tip forward again, putting as much force as I can muster against the edge of the antique locking mechanism. The humidity has swollen the wood, so the latching is sporadic. It gives way, with my determined effort and some marring on both our parts. I fall forward, as anticipated. Now there is nothing to do but wait. The smoke curls up, and I am faced with the possibility of igniting before I am able to be used again. To provide help in the form of shelter… my greatest joy and privilege.

I am fortunate. The flames are slowed by their struggle against the dense paper which, I suspect, may be slightly damp, and the smoke is abundant. It reaches the sensor and trips an audible alarm. Then it happens. The water falls down from the ceiling. It has been there for some time, and I rebel against the stagnation, freeing the water from its reserves. It is a near thing, the closest I have felt to rain in quite some time, but I am furled, and it disappoints.

I knew my client would arrive with great haste, and suddenly there he is.

The man's eyes take in my state, the outlet, the papers, and then, to my abject horror, he uses the copy of the London Financial Times tucked beneath his arm as a makeshift head-covering, stepping over me, and disabling the alarm. The reset code, oddly enough, seems to correspond to his measurements.

"I have always held that umbrella use should be a distinctly open-air pastime," he says, as he walks back to the doorway and kneels down beside me. "Clever. I was wondering how you would manage to get me to retrieve you." My canopy gapes open.

"My name is Mycroft Holmes. It is my business to know what other people do not know. A sentient umbrella. When you eliminate the impossible, whatever remains, however improbable, must be the truth. I need to keep an eye on you. Umbrellas are never to be entirely trusted. Not the best of them."

Had I the power of speech, I would have paused to argue over that atrocious statement.

"And you also have the grand gift of silence. While that is fairly typical of an umbrella, it does make you quite invaluable as a companion. There's a storm coming, such a wind as never blew on

England yet. It will be cold and bitter, and a good many umbrellas may wither before its blast. You're an umbrella. In fact, I'd say you're a high-functioning parapluie. You've seen a lot of rain, violent storms. Shall we see some more, then?"

I tremble ever so slightly as he places me in his hands, stopping to lightly stroke the damaged wood of my handle, and all I can think is *Oh, God, yes.*

It Could Have Been Worse
By Les Moskowitz

Family relationships in the Canon are *strange*.

In *Hound of the Baskervilles*, we learn that Jack Stapleton's "sister" was really his wife.

In *Priory School*, we learn that James Wilder, the Duke's secretary was really his son.

In *Copper Beeches*, we read of parents who imprisoned their daughter.

Sussex Vampire is about a family in which a young boy attempts to poison his baby brother.

And perhaps, the worst, *A Case of Identity*, in which Mary Sutherland's future husband is really her step-father.

BUT IT COULD HAVE BEEN WORSE!

Before the marriage of James Windibank to Mary Sutherland's mother, it would have been natural for the two families to meet. And perhaps, when James Windibank's father met Mary Sutherland, they, too, might have fallen in love and also gotten married.

What would that have done?

1. James Windibank, married to Mary Sutherland's mother became Mary Sutherland's step-father. (In the sake of brevity, I'm now going to eliminate the "step-" prefix)
2. Mary Sutherland, married to James Windibank's father became James Windibank's mother. So Mary was both Windibank's daughter and his mother.
3. And it gets worse.
4. Since Mary is James Windibank's mother, her mother became James Windibank's grandmother.
5. And the husband of Mary Sutherland's mother became James Windibank's grandfather.

But the husband of Mary Sutherland's mother was James Windibank. So, from the above statement (4), James Windibank was his own grandfather.

And it doesn't get any worse than that!

Holmes and Watson in the 'Uncanny Decade'
by Chris Aarnes Bakkane

Being an avid lover of different interpretations and adaptations of Sherlock Holmes, I've long been toying with the idea to write or create one of my own. Unfortunately, I never felt confident enough to do Sir Arthur Conan Doyle's characters justice and always feared critique from the older and 'elite' Holmesians for not doing it right or ruining the characters and stories. But then, one night during a particular strenuous writing session for my master thesis in 2019, the assuring words of Doyle to actor William Gillette rung in my ears: "Marry him, kill him, do whatever you like with him!" And that's when the comic *Project Red Diamond* was born.

The general idea is that after returning from the war in Vietnam, a weary and injured John H. Watson leaves his small hometown in America to England to get in touch with his British family roots and to – hopefully – start a new life. Later, when coming in contact with his childhood friend Mike Stamford, Watson travels to London with new, but uncertain prospects and attempts to adapt to everyday living in the bustling big city. But after a visit to Stamford's workplace, St. Bartholomew's Hospital, Watson has a fateful meeting with an eccentric young man, Sherlock Holmes, that would prove to change his life - in more ways than one - forever…

For me it was imperative that I had to adapt *A Study in Scarlet*, but to alter the story enough to fit within the new decade. And the reason for choosing the 1970s is that I have a lot of love for it. Not only for the aesthetics and fashion of the period, but also popular culture like film and music. But the decade was also important when it came to cultural and political change in the West. I hadn't seen any adaptation placing Holmes and Watson in this particular decade, so I felt I had to give it a go and have some fun doing it, but also aim to tackle the more problematic cultural and societal aspects of the decade when it comes to race, gender and particularly sexuality. Taking place in London during the 1970s, the "Me decade", *Project Red Diamond* shifts its focus more to the characters' lives and struggles living in a radically changing world riddled with the restrictions from decades past. The time for conformity is over, which both Holmes and Watson will learn with the help from each other and from the people around them. As of 2020 the plans for *Project Red Diamond* are in motion, but there's still a lot of planning, writing and sketching ahead before finishing the issue. But it's a passion project, and I'll do everything in my power to bring it to life in the next 2-3 years. Hopefully other will be interested in the future endeavours of 1970s Holmes and Watson.

The Resurrection Of Sherlock Holmes
By Roger Johnson

In '93 a tragic rumour
put readers in a frantic humour.
Throughout the land the sad news spread –
Alas, the great detective's dead!

Slow-witted persons scratched their domes.
What – dead? You can't mean Sherlock Holmes!
If this is true then Conan Doyle
ought to be flogged, or boiled in oil!

How could he? We're his devotees!
We look to him in times like these
to be gripped by a thrilling story –
droll perhaps, or maybe gory –
a tale of Sherlock Holmes's glory...

We're not exceptionally dim,
but we'd come to rely on him
for quality and reassurance.
And this – this is beyond endurance!

Was Sherlock as a man defective?
Perhaps – but still, as a detective
no sleuth was ever more effective!

And now there'll be no more adventures –
jewels in geese, men flinging dentures,
vanished bridegrooms, business fakes,
royal crowns and vicious snakes.

No more we'll savour at our leisure
crooked men, exotic treasure,
ancient rituals, orange pips,
abducted horses, convict ships,
severed ears and twisted lips.

Sherlock was the perfect sleuth,
pre-eminent, and that's the truth.
Is there one to match this man?
There's not, alas, for no one can.
How did this sad thing come to be –
and who's this chap Mor-eye-ar-tee?

Yes, what of that felonious party,
whose name's correctly Moriarty?
The professor – what of him?
Well, James – or did they call him Jim? –
like Holmes had passed life's every test,
but he was worst where Holmes was best.

Of course, he was a genius – hence
I mean "worst" in the moral sense.
He was the evil mastermind,
the planning genius behind
every crime gone undetected,
and even evils unsuspected.

As soon as Holmes became aware,
no time or effort did he spare.
For years the great detective worked
(for, as you know, he never shirked)
to find the brains behind each misdeed,
who organised that deed and this deed.

A soldier, or a toff, perhaps...
Who else might lead those crooked chaps
to blackmail, murder, robbery?
An academic...? It would be
a practical and novel twist!

Yes, this is what the cops have missed –
the master crook's a scientist!

The impact of his crimes is tragic,
but oh, such skill! It seems like magic.
So potent has this villain grown,
yet somehow he remains unknown.
In all the chronicles of crime
there's been no genius so sublime.

There's no such thing as a magician,
therefore our man's a math'matician.
His web, which stretches all through Lundun,
is dangerous and must be undone.
So reasoned Holmes, and thus began
an exploit worthy of the man.

By taking many a perilous route
through areas of ill repute –
opium dens and seedy pubs,
knocking shops and gambling clubs,
Chinatown and Wapping Stairs,
where constables patrol in pairs –
Holmes followed greater clues and lesser,
and traced them to the ex-Professor.

But then, you know, the enemy
was no less sapient than he.
His morals scored a big fat zero,
but he was canny, like our hero,
and very soon this evildoer
(whose home by rights should be a sewer)
became aware there was a snooper,
and even in a thick pea-souper
he didn't have to think too hard
to know it wasn't Scotland Yard.

Moriarty grasped the fact
the author of that hostile act,
that devious detective feat,
was Sherlock Holmes of Baker Street.
So Holmes worked out a cunning scheme
to shatter the Professor's dream,
arrest the leader and his gang,
and see that every one should hang.

Meanwhile the devious master cad
tried to frighten our brave lad –
sending thugs to tan his hide,
and thump him till he nearly died,
attempt to run the poor chap down
in the streets of London town,
and drop bricks from a lofty roof –
while Moriarty stayed aloof.

The lack of serious effect
caused the Professor to reflect
that Holmes was far too circumspect –
so he resolved to be direct.

Away to Baker Street he wandered,
where Sherlock sat and gently pondered,
now that his task was almost done.
The blackguard entered 221
And all in silence climbed the stair
to Holmes's flat - or den - or lair.

Then gently, with the slightest sound,
the door unclosed – and Holmes looked round.
There stood the wily pedagogue,
that baneful spawn of mist and fog.

Pale, clean-shaven, tall and thin,
his forehead large, his eyes sunk in
and glittering, their hue obsidian –
and worse, with curious ophidian
effect his white face oscillated,
almost as though it indicated
the restless nature of his mind –
and yet his voice was almost kind:

"I thought that you would look more highbrow."
At this Holmes raised a weary eyebrow,
and stood alert, with visage grim.
The other merely looked at him
and spoke as to an erring son,
"You're fingering a loaded gun,
inside" – he added with a frown –
"the pocket of your dressing-gown.
Or – goodness gracious, Holmes! how dreamy!
Can it be you're pleased to see me?
Whichever, it's a dangerous move,
and one of which I disapprove."

Holmes placed his pistol on the table,
but close to hand, so he'd be able
to use it, should occasion be
born of sad necessity.

Said James, "It seems you don't know me."
"Not so," said Holmes. "I'm sure you see
I know you very well, you crook.
In fact I read you like a book."

"Alas," the other said, "it's sad.
I'm hampered in my plans so bad-
ly by your interference,
what I need's your disappearance –
and that would cause me grief, you know.
Don't smile! I tell you it is so."

Moriarty briefly sighed.
"You'll be found washed up on the tide,
unless you're wise and step aside."
"I'm used to danger," Holmes replied.

The ex-professor's face was wry.
"Well, none can say I didn't try.
Sherlock, you're a clever man,
but you can't beat me – no one can.
If by chance I come to grief,
don't fancy you will find relief.
Hark well, for what I say is true:
I'll bring destruction down on you!"

Said Holmes, "Trust me, I'd welcome death
if it meant you'd drawn your last breath."
The other turned and took his leave,
but Sherlock Holmes felt no reprieve.

The prof departed, choked with choler
and Holmes would bet his bottom dollar
that such a mood, malign and sore,
betokened only one thing – war.

After this grim face-to-face
he toddled round to Watson's place
and, hardly ere a word was uttered,
made sure the room was safely shuttered,
then in that quiet solitude
advised his old friend how things stude.

"Monday next's the fateful day.
That's when the police will say,
'Mr. Holmes, we've got them all –
Every one. It's quite a haul.
Moriarty and his gang
all rounded up, the whole shebang.'"

The doctor's wife was on a visit.
Holmes cried, "Watson, that's exquisite!
My dear chap, if that is so
I hope that you'll agree to go
sur le Continong with me.
Precisely where? Just wait and see."

Then quietly Holmes slipped away,
and at an early hour next day,
with a minimum of fuss,
by a route circuituss,
Watson, like a doughty warrior,
took a cab-ride to Victorria.

The train was in, no time to spare –
but where was Holmes? Holmes wasn't there!
Just an old Italian priest,
evidently not the least
acquainted with the English tongue
and possibly quite highly strung.

Alone by the engaged compartment
waiting, poor old Watson's heart went
thump thump, till the whistle sounded
and the train was outward bounded.

Still no sign of Holmes! Oh dear.
He's certainly said he'd be here,
thought Watson – yes, Holmes made that clear.
But then a quiet familiar voice
said, "My dear Watson!" Ha! Rejoice!

You might think Watson used some choice
expressions at this devious trick
(he had, we know, been worried sick)
but no, the fact is he was too
relieved and happy so to do.

You've guessed it. The ecclesiastic
was, though it may seem fantastic,
Holmes himself. His great disguise
had pulled the wool o'er Watson's eyes –
and Moriarty's eyes, let's hope.
They'd put him off the scent. Yup? Nope!

For peering out along the platform,
Holmes exclaimed, "There! D'you see that form?
The tall man, pushing through the throng?
That's he. It didn't take him long!

No doubt he had men watching you –
but then it's just what I should do."

"Ah, well," said Watson, "never mind.
The train's pulled out on time, I find.
Every cloud is silver-lined –
and we have left him far behind."

Said Holmes, "My far too trusting friend,
It seems you do not comprehend
that this man's brain is really good,
which means he'll do just what I should."

"What's that?" asked Watson. "Tell me plain!"
"Why, he'll engage a special train,
and if he catches us at Dover
our bold adventure will be over."

Watson thought and then suggested,
"Why not have the man arrested?"
"That," said Holmes, "would surely spoil
three months of dedicated toil –
All the gang would disappear.
No, we must play it cool, I fear.

"At Canterbury we'll get off,
and then the wicked scheming prof
will follow this train on to Dover.
Meanwhile we shall be in clover –

We'll make our way from Canter-berry
to Newhaven, to catch the ferry."

And so they did. They crossed to France
over the Channel's blue expanse,
and landed safely at Dieppe,
much refreshed and full of pep.

Brussels, Strasbourg – on they went,
quite as if on pleasure bent,
giving Scotland Yard a free hand

Holmes telegraphed the London cops
to check they'd pull out all the stops,
to break up the illegal party,
arrest the gang – and Moriarty.
Then he breathed a worried sigh
and waited for the cops' reply.

It came on Monday. Eagerly
Holmes opened it, agog to see.
Alas, the tidings were not good,
for things had not gone as they should.

True, the gang had all been took,
but Moriarty, cunning crook,
had got away and ventured forth
to stalk Holmes and appease his wrawth.

Said Holmes, "The man is on my track.
I think, old friend, you'd best go back,
for I'm an unsafe chap to be with –
a fact I'm sure that you'll agree with."

"Nonsense!" Watson cried. "Old fellow,
if you imagine I'd turn yellow
then think again! I've served the Queen,
and many dangers have I seen,
where red blood stained the desert sand
at the battle of Mai-wand."

So off they went, not caring where,
Holmes and Watson, free as air,
till faced with scenery spectacular
Holmes remarked in tones oracular:
"Mountains, lakes – who owns these bits o' land?
Where's Baedeker? Ah! We're in Switzerland!

"I suggest then that we sally
forth along the river valley
as far as Leuk, then o'er the Gemmi
to where I think we may be semi-
safe." And so they made their way
on past the gloomy Daubensee.

The prof would follow, he'd no doubt,
so still Holmes kept a sharp look out.
And sure enough, beside the lake
a great rock clattered in their wake
down from the height, just missing him
and plunging o'er the water's brim.

Yet Sherlock didn't seem unhappy.
His conversation still was snappy.
"My dear old fellow, it is plain
to me that I've not lived in vain.

"To free the world of Moriarty,
I'd bid my own career a hearty
farewell. I think that your book
of memoirs closes when that crook
is killed or captured." On they strode
along the rocky mountain road,
till as the skies began to darken
they reached the town of Interlaken.

From thence these stalwart Englishmen
made their way to Meiringen.

They stayed the night at the hotel
Englischer Hof (we know it well)
then off on the ensuing day -
their destination, Rosen-lay.

The landlord Steiler told them this:
"There's one sight that you must not miss.
See the falls of Reichenbach
before the evening gets too dach."

It is indeed a fearful place.
They pondered, each with solemn face,
awestruck upon the great abyss
where plunging waters roar and hiss.

They turned to leave, but fortune had
a different plan. A young Swiss lad
came with a message to implore
the doctor to return once more
and treat an English woman who -
about to bid the world adieu -
required an English doc with gumption
to ease the pain of her consumption.

Watson could not ignore the plea,
and taking leave of Sherlock, he
went down the mountain speedily.
Arriving at the hostelry
he blurted, out of breath and terse,
"I trust, Herr Steiler, she's no worse?"

But no, there was no dying lady.
At once things looked distinctly shady.

"As for the fateful begging note,"
said Steiler, "I think he who wrote
it was a tall thin Englishman..."
Watson turned, and off he ran
from the house of Peter Steiler,
fast as an Olympic miler.

Two more hours elapsed before
he fetched up at the falls once more.
There was Holmes's Alpine-stock,
leaning still against a rock.

Alas, no sign of Holmes himself
on that narrow rocky shelf.
Watson shouted, all in vain.
Only echoes came again.

The Swiss lad too had disappeared.
Watson thought, "It's as I feared.
He was Moriarty's minion,
sent, it is my firm opinion,
to separate me from my friend –
and oh, alas! to what foul end?"

A note from Sherlock proved to be
all the explanation he
would get. Holmes knew the young Swiss boy
was probably the prof's decoy,
but let his friend depart, in hope
that Moriarty soon would lope
on to that narrow rocky way
and, so to speak, make Holmes's day.

Experts scrutinised the spot
and soon decided there was not
the slightest doubt what had transpired.
Both those mighty men desired
to end the other fellow's life,
and also end their bitter strife,
But they were closely matched, and so
the chances were that both would go.

And that's what Doyle's readers read.
Watson thought his friend was dead –
so did the public. Some believe
that men wore black bands on their sleeve.

Letters certainly were sent
to ask the author what he meant
by killing Britain's fav'rite sleuth –
and some of them were quite uncouth.
One lady wrote to him, "You brute!"
Doyle thought that one was rather cute.

The public mourned for eight more years –
"Great Holmes is dead. Let flow your tears!"
Then an announcement in The Strand
caused exultation through the land.

"Just read this tale!" ran the directive.
"Another case for the detective –
The Hound of the Baskervilles!"
The title gave them pleasant chills,
and when the first instalment came
they eagerly devoured the same.

In fact, the readers lapped it up,
delighted to be sold a pup!

Sherlock Holmes: The Adventure of Gloria Scott
By M L Duffy

I never knew which Sherlock Holmes I would find when I went downstairs for breakfast. Would I find the energetic sleuth or active researcher or a long streak sprawled on our settee? On a good day, he'd entertain me with his often hilarious critiques of television crime drama. On bad days he'd lack the energy to binge-watch. I didn't have to wait long this breezy March morning to discover which version would appear.

The pots of daffodils on the balcony, swaying like demented street-dancers, put a smile on my face as I made my first pot of tea of the day. My smile faltered as Holmes trudged into view at the kitchen door. A blonde wig hung loosely around his angular face, the eye shadow matching the sparkly blue blouse sitting above a denim skirt. Our curtain pelmets contained more fabric than the skirt! Thick black tights and black knee-high boots completed his ensemble.

'John, I can hear cogs grating. Either you're thinking, or the central heating boiler just kicked in,' Holmes said.

'It's fine by me. Just… unexpected.'

Why Holmes surprises me, after four months of flat-sharing with him, is still the biggest mystery of all.

'Pour me a cuppa. I've spent all night drinking that low-alcohol lager muck in a night-club,' he said.

'Not had a good night out, then.'

'All in a good cause, I was following someone, but it really didn't improve the taste any,' he said, tottering into the living room. The leather cushions exhaled as he collapsed heavily on to the settee. 'You've heard me mention Trevor?'

I was sure I hadn't. In fact, I'm sure Holmes often has entire conversations with me in my absence.

'Name doesn't ring any bells,' I called back.

'It was my first case. Trev was a friend at Uni.'

'He was your first client?'

He'd piqued my interest. There hadn't been a right time to ask him about his past without feeling it would come off as being nosy.

'Not exactly,' Holmes said. 'His father was the first criminal I detected.'

'What did he do?' I asked, handing him the steaming mug. It struck me that exposing his friend's father as a criminal must have made for a short friendship.

'Trevor, Trev's father, an investment banking clerk, took money from an elderly woman's account. He'd been convinced to invest it in a scheme for a fast high-profit return. He was scammed,' Holmes continued.

'What?'

'Totally stitched up. Lost the lot and couldn't replace it before the audit. He had no proof he'd been conned. He fled abroad under a false identity and only returned to England some twenty years later. He lived a quiet life in fear of being recognised. And it killed him. He suffered a fatal heart attack. He left a letter to his son to be opened only after his death. Made a full confession.'

'That must have been a terrible shock for your friend,' I said, crossing the room to the desk. I sat cradling my tea.

'Trev was devastated. He'd recently lost his dad and found his comfortable life in a big old manor house on the Norfolk Broads was built on theft, deception, and lies.'

'Did you find the scammer?'

'It took months but, by the time I'd convinced the police to look into it, he'd slipped away. Since he knows what I look like, it has called for subterfuge.' He indicated his disguise with a languid hand.

We sat in silence for a moment, Holmes relishing his tea. I wondered if he'd dropped out of university to spend months trying to prove his father's friend had been a victim, and not simply a common thief.

He glanced at the rectangular ivory-white dial of a dainty gold bracelet-watch on his wrist. It cast a dancing beam of warm light across the rug.

'My first appointment is in twelve minutes,' he said

He unzipped the boots, tugged them off. 'Double top for the match.' He aimed them, first one then the other, at the brass coal scuttle by the fireside. Both boots clanged into the bucket.

An impish smile curled his lips. A fiend for keeping me in suspense, he liked to surprise me with a dramatic flourish.

'You've cheered up. What's the secret?' I smiled.

'I've found the scammer again. He's now calling himself Steffan Leon. I followed him from a restaurant to a nightclub last night.'

'Well done. They say patience is a virtue - living proof.' I grinned.

'I say found. More he's been delivered to me. My client, Anita Tyndall, came to me worried about her man-friend's behaviour. Nearly broke the bell, she was in such a state. Pounding the pavement followed by insistent leaning on the bell is always a sign of a heart in anguish.'

'Really? Sorry, go on.'

'She's the manager of a charity's donations department. A woman, Mrs. Hoxley, contacted her about making a hefty donation. Miss Tyndall became concerned when her man-friend, Steffan Leon, contacted Mrs. Hoxley off his own bat without telling her. He obtained Mrs. Hoxley's email address from Miss Tyndall's laptop.'

Holmes swigged a mouthful of tea.

'Oh,' I said. 'Invasion of privacy. Did she give him her password?'

'She didn't. He pried into her business affairs. And, since it was the last straw as far as she was concerned, she came to me with her suspicions.'

'She suspected Steffan Leon of what?'

'Being disingenuous, meddling, controlling behaviour, possibly stalking her, worming his way into her confidence, toying with her heart.'

I felt my eyebrows losing themselves in my hairline.

'Poor woman,' I said. 'That's quite a litany of sins.'

'I don't normally do background checks, there are other agencies for that. I put her on to one. Steffan Leon didn't check out. I recognised him from a photograph as the man who conned Trev's father. I instructed Mrs. Hoxley to meet Leon last night to obtain evidence. Last night wasn't a wild success, but the game isn't over yet.'

Holmes finished his tea and, with a twinkle in his eyes, he padded off to his bedroom, a glorified large closet furnished with his single bed and a massive bank of storage cupboards, which adjoins our living-room. He returned, within a few minutes, in his usual slim-fitting black jeans and a dark blue shirt, his dark hair tamed for the moment.

'That was a quick change,' I said.

'I kept something back from you,' he said, sitting to face me. 'This is not out of a wish to deceive you.'

I drained my cup, my brain fizzing with curiosity outweighing a smattering of dread. What was so terrible that he felt compelled to dump it on me now merely minutes before his eight-thirty appointment?

'You know my methods. I see the bigger picture from observing small details. Details that practically everyone else fails to notice,' he continued.

'Yes.'

'It was my hobby when I was at university. What I chose not to tell you, until now, was of my involvement in a later case for a student, Rodney Mossgrave. His family performs the Mossgrave Ritual when the house and fortune pass to the next heir.'

'Right.'

'I can't tell you why the ritual had no effect on Rodney but affected me.' His face was serious. 'I gained a little useful ability from that. One is a transformation of appearance.'

'This was a theatrical family? Stage-craft.'

'You might call it that or witch-craft.' He smiled faintly.

'I remember saying the day we met, it was a good thing they no longer burned witches. I was astounded how you knew half my life story just from observing details. Very clever.'

Holmes blushed like a maiden in one of the bodice-ripper novels that Mrs. Hudson is fond of devouring.

'They hanged witches in England actually, but that's people for you,' he said. 'Terrified of things they can't explain.'

'Things that look like magic.'

'Absolutely.'

'I've seen level-headed soldiers approach diagnostic hospital machinery with trepidation.'

'Knew you would understand,' Holmes said, and another a glimmer of a smile escaped his grasp.

I should say now I completely failed to understand what he was on about, but I thought no more about his confession because the front doorbell pealed.

'That's Mrs. Hoxley,' he said, pulling a face worthy of Christopher Lee with fangs. He crossed his forefingers at arm's length, suggesting he expected a vampire to be calling in for his advice.

I jogged downstairs. The woman on the doorstep possessed several attractive attributes. Nature had been kind, or her plastic surgeon must holiday in the Bahamas on his income. I expected a melodic voice to match.

'I'm Grace Hoxley, to see Sherlock Holmes,' she announced. Her voice befitted a bear suffering from haemorrhoids. She thrust her black umbrella at me. 'My appointment is for half-past eight.'

She altered her tone to a lilt and put on airs, pronouncing it as "huff pust aight." It took effort from me to swallow a grimace. 'He's expecting you, Mrs. Hoxley, if you'd like to go upstairs.'

I consigned her brolly to the hall-stand and wondered where she'd parked her broomstick as she bustled past me. I closed the door and followed her upstairs.

Holmes, now standing at the fireplace, had been busy. Piles of magazines and newspapers and a cardboard box took up the seats, except for the sofa and office chair. I made to go up to my bedroom to give my friend privacy with his client as usual.

'John, stay if you don't mind. Please.'

Resuming my place at the desk, I swiveled the chair to face inward.

'Thank you for coming, Mrs. Hoxley, have a seat,' Holmes said. 'The bull pup vacated the settee a moment ago.'

I frowned at the mention of a dog we don't have.

'I'll stand, thank you.' she replied, using her put-on voice. 'I'm sure you are busy, as am I.' She bristled at me or the confetti of newspaper clippings scattered on the desk. I formed the opinion that life displeased her at every turn.

'Mr. Holmes, I afforded you the perfect opportunity to catch that frightful schemer last night, and you failed. What do you intend to do about this now?'

'Would you prefer me to boil Mr. Leon alive in front of you or just give you his head on a spike?'

I stifled a laugh.

'I wish him caught and imprisoned,' she replied.

'Then follow my advice. I asked you to take a friend to act as a witness last night.'

'He specified that he preferred to meet me, alone, in a congenial atmosphere. Maison Dupont was the ideal restaurant.'

'For Leon, yes. That's why he suggested it.' Holmes paused, tight-lipped, and cast me an unreadable glance. 'Mrs. Hoxley, please follow my advice when you contact him. Arrange for him to meet, where I choose, an associate of yours who wishes to invest in his project. I will supply the friend.'

'And if he refuses?'

'He won't. Tell him your business associate, Fahima Al Khasela, wishes to invest a quarter of a million pounds of her father's money, in cash. Mr. Leon would meet someone in Shadrow's Finger-lickin' Chicken Shack to get his hands on that amount.'

'Mr. Holmes!'

'Oh, you know Shadrow's. Nasty business with those cockroaches, John. Anyway, Mrs. Hoxley, please inform Mr. Leon that Fahima will meet him in the Chartwell Claremont Grand Hotel, Holborn, tonight at nine-o-clock before she leaves London. Book a triple bed suite, and I'll see you're reimbursed by the Victim Compensation Scheme. Do this, and I will catch him in the act.' He glanced at the clock, his face registering sudden horror. 'I have another appointment. Tempus fugits so fast when you're having fun.'

'I had to cancel a meeting to be here,' she complained to me as she flounced out.

'Someone got out of bed on the wrong side this morning.' I said, after the front door banged shut.

'She's peeved because the soup slopped in her lap.'
'That's as clear as mud.'

'So was the soup.' He took the weight off his feet. 'I asked Mrs. Hoxley to meet Steffan Leon in a quiet place where I could catch him attempting to make her sign five-hundred thousand pounds over to him. I dressed as a waitress. The display of tender emotions was sickening. She was hanging on his every word. He was all over her. The pen was poised in her hand, can you believe? I saved her by dropping soup on the documents, it dribbled into her lap. Her dress was a Galliana Fawcett number.'

I nodded. It was a huge brand name in the fashion world. And expensive. 'She's got a few bob, then.'

'More money than sense,' he muttered. He stuck out his tongue as if he couldn't lose the taste of the maligned lager. 'Another pot of tea, I think.'

Holmes restored his clutter to the floor while I filled his beverage request. A few minutes later, Mrs. Hudson answered the front door. The sound of footsteps on the stairs increased in volume. The client, a woman with brown hair framing rounded features, tapped on our open door.

Holmes offered her a seat. 'Miss Anita Tyndall, this is my friend, Doctor Watson. He should hear about Mr. Leon from you. Tea?'

'Anita, please. No tea, thanks, I had one in a café on the way here.'

We tilted our heads at each other before she took a chair and clenched her hands together on the lap of her powder-blue trouser-suit.

'It's crazy.' She sighed. 'I met Steffan Leon at a charity auction. I'm a homeless person's charity fund-raising manager. He was charming and very attentive. We dated for several weeks. I was flattered. He obviously had money, but he wasn't put off that I lived in a houseboat.'

I nodded.

'Then I discovered he'd been on my laptop,' Anita said. 'He used my email to arrange to meet Grace Hoxley, a new client of mine, about her plans to make a generous donation. Five hundred thousand pounds. He passed it off as just trying to help because he had influence, and said he hadn't told me because he wanted it to be a surprise. The rotten liar.'

Anita wrung her hands to white knuckles and took a lungful of air. 'Ooh, that man, I want to give him a piece of my mind. Tansy knew he was no good. Tansy's my dog. She wanted to be friendly, but he didn't. He claimed he was nervous around dogs because he was bitten as a child. One morning they were both on deck, I went up by chance, and there was a splash. It's not like Tansy to jump in the water without me there. She's obedience trained. It's my hobby competing with her, you see. Well, she was swimming to the steps when I looked over the side.'

Anita paused, checking Holmes' face. 'I'm sure he pushed Tansy into the water. He said she jumped in after a duck. It'd be the first time ever. I gave him the benefit of the doubt but Tansy didn't trust him after that.'

Holmes said, 'Last night's plan failed due to circumstances beyond my control. A second attempt will be made tonight. I followed Leon until seven this morning.'

'I see. Yes, he turned up at my boat about half-past seven. There's worse news, I'm afraid. He grabbed my laptop and put a password on it. He's got control of everything now.'

'It'll be over soon,' Holmes said. 'You're booked into a hotel and removed the battery from your phone?'

'Yes.' She gave him the name of the hotel. 'He won't be able to see where I am. I left Tansy with a friend. She's safe.'

'You've nothing to worry about, then,' Holmes said, radiating confidence.

Anita sallied out with a lighter step and a smile.

His expression became tense. The show of confidence was not a true reflection of his feelings. 'I could use your help, John.'

'Of course,' I replied.

Holmes and I spent the day gathering items he needed, including hiring me a suit for the evening. At seven, he donned a porter's uniform and sauntered into the Holborn hotel through the back door. He sent me to a council housing estate. The kid-on-a-too-small-bicycle popping wheelies and three bored youths- sitting-on-a-low-brick-wall sort of council estate. They eyed me with suspicion as I rapped on the door of the flat.

The flat's occupant, my height and gruff peered out. 'We don't want any,' he said with Yorkshire vowels from the dark recess of a grubby grey hoodie.

'You want me. I'm James Hill Barton,' I answered as Holmes had instructed.

'Brad Shaw,' he said, easing his shoulders. 'Come in and meet our, er, employer.' I stepped in, and he closed the door. 'Give me five mins to get changed,' he added.

A young woman wearing a dove-grey skirt and blouse, glittering with gold and diamond jewellery, floated into the hallway.

'Ello, John. Detective Sergeant Sharanjit Mepal,' she introduced herself in an East End accent. 'Sharan, off duty.' She gave me a twirl and a smile. 'Tonight, I'm Fahima Al Khaseltzer. Daughter of a filthy rich criminal wishing to launder a quarter of a million pounds of dirty money.'

'Sherlock said the name was Fahima Al Khasela,' I queried.

'It is. I'm joking.' She grinned. 'Mr. Leon's gonna need something to settle his stomach when we arrest him.'

'Right,' I replied, laughing at her gallows humour.

'You and your colleague, Brad, will do the talking for me. I don't shake hands or speak English.' She grinned again. 'Not until I give Leon the standard Met greeting of 'Oi, you little scrote, you're nicked."

Brad Shaw returned wearing a made-to-measure Savile Row suit. He handed me a transmitter watch and a transparent earpiece. 'Now that's us tooled up,' he said after we'd fitted ourselves with the gadgets, 'I'll bring the car.'

The car, an Aston Martin, like Brad's suit, didn't look remotely like it'd been hired for the occasion. Rain streamed down the windows of the Aston as we crawled through traffic to the Grand Hotel.

Like secret agents, I moved to the hotel doors while Brad opened the passenger door for Sharan and held an umbrella up ready. She emerged, wearing a headscarf and dark glasses, like a film-star into the drizzle. The car valet took the keys and drove away.

Someone had denuded Italy of marble to furnish the hotel foyer. Another bright spark had decided the heating should recreate desert conditions. I sweltered until my hair was damp. My shirt collar fought my tie for the pleasure of strangling me as we escorted our faux VIP up to her eyry on the top floor.

After the lift doors swished open, we found ourselves facing a slender, elderly man with a sharp nose, grey hair, and fierce, slanting eyebrows. He had two bull-necked bodyguards in tow. They were a matched pair for sour expressions. A blue suit stretched taut, torturing the buttons, over a barrel chest on one. A green tie garroted the other. Green Tie's nose looked to have been rearranged by a shovel at some point in his career. I pegged the bodyguards as shouty ex-forces types, the sort of men happier kicking down doors than being kept on a tight leash forced to be polite and invisible while babysitting their belligerent VIP. Side-stepping around them, we followed Brad soundlessly along the thickly carpeted corridor. He swiped the key-card and let us into the suite.

'Oooh,' Sharan cooed at the extravaganza of green, pink, and gold.

Holmes, looking out of the panoramic window at the twinkling city lights, nodded. 'We'll know by nine if Steffan Leon takes the bait. DI Lestrade inserted a DC on the reception desk.'

'DC Simon Myers. He'll report as soon as Leon shows his face,' Sharan confirmed. She produced a pack of playing cards from her shoulder bag and held them up, waggling them like a trophy.

The hands moved like slugs around the clock on the wall. I felt bilious being surrounded by a sea of green flocked wallpaper as the sea-slugs passed nine-forty. Holmes, who had been wearing out the carpet, pacing for fifteen minutes, halted abruptly.

'Ah. I see it now,' he said. 'Grace Hoxley is in on it, and not just in on it, she is the master-mind. Steffan Leon is her accomplice. How did I not see that before?'

Brad's cards slapped on the table.

'Can't be,' Sharan answered.

More like none of us wanted it to be true. I felt appalled that the woman knew his whole plan.

'How do you know, Sherlock?' I asked for Sharan's benefit.

'Grace Hoxley ignored my advice to take a witness to the restaurant. She was on the point of signing documents when I prevented it. The ploy was to show Anita that her employer's funds would be safe with Leon after Hoxley supposedly signed over funds to him, and would then report making a quick profit to her. Leon set Anita up for stealing from her employers, being tricked into thinking it was safe.'

'It's what they did before. To Trev's father,' I said.

'But Mrs. Hoxley paid for this suite,' Sharan argued.

'She wears Galliana Fawcett, she's conned people out of who knows how many millions. Four hundred quid for a suite's nothing to her.' Holmes replied.

His eyes burned bright. 'Her power is on the decline,' he rapped out. 'Tell Lestrade she needs to watch the airports for her. Hoxley knows the game is up, she'll ditch Leon.'

'Brad, come with me to reception,' Sharan said, making for the door. 'Myers has a radio to update the boss.'

Brad hurried after her.

'Is Brad Shaw the Job?' I asked as Holmes turned back to the window.

'He's not police. He did the background check on Leon. Can you shush, I'm trying to think. Why did Leon go to a nightclub?'

'He couldn't go back to Anita's in case the police were there?'

'No, no, why a night-club?'

'Did he talk to or meet someone?'

'No.'

Out of ideas, I buttoned it. The reflection in the glass was his familiar one with a faraway, studious look in his eyes. Then his face lit again, and he pivoted on his heel.

'That's it. He didn't go for the social life. What if he avoided returning to his hotel because he'd already conned someone? Someone dangerous. What if he was hiding in a crowd, surrounding himself with people for safety?'

'I thought snakes slithered down holes.'

'You didn't see the night-club!'

We exchanged brief smiles before Holmes snatched his coat from the chair. He swept us out and sprinted down the corridor. 'Anita Tyndall's in great danger,' he said, jabbing the lift call button.

My stomach sat in my throat before the lift plummeted twenty floors.

'I hate guessing,' he said. 'It's dangerous to do. But let's say Hoxley and Leon stole from someone big and scary. What would you do if you were an angry gangster with a couple of goons with guns?'

I thought of the VIP with eyebrows and his surly minders.

'You'd want to get your money back.'

'The fast way, with a vengeance as a cold side dish, is to grab Leon's girlfriend and hold her to ransom.'

'They wouldn't shoot Anita. They'd lose the leverage of having her as a hostage by killing her.'

'Doesn't mean they wouldn't rough her up to obtain information. Info she doesn't have. The greater danger is if she tells them she's also a victim. That makes her worthless to them. They're hardly going to apologise to her after slapping her around and put her in a taxi.'

I left the lift side-on with Holmes on my heels and found the foyer heavily populated by guests. Our old friends Blue Goon and Green Tie stood with their eyes on two couples. They were still imitating dogs licking nettles. DC Myers, behind the reception desk, looked the part of a receptionist in a dark green uniform with brass buttons. Sharan, in front of the counter, spoke into Myers' police issue radio.

'Mind your backs. Coming through,' Holmes called out.
Plenty gawped at the porter being chased by a minder, but nobody moved. We elbowed our way through the patrons busily downing drinks.

Coiffured heads turned as Holmes knocked into an elderly man and a woman in a gaudy dress. Her champagne flew into the face of her six-hundred-quid-sort-of- hairdo female companion. Posh Hair lady's mascara ran down her face and she smeared it into a cryptic code only pandas could decipher.

'Sorry. Emergency,' I said to them.

I recognised the elderly man when I saw his bushy eyebrows. He surged forward, a tidal wave of outraged flesh. Screeching, 'Who are you? Who?' like an owl, he seized Holmes' sleeve.

'Okay, hands off,' I said, stepping in to stop the man interfering. Anita was in danger; Holmes didn't need his attention diverting.

Owl Man raised his gnarled, bony fist. Blue Goon flung himself at me. I braced for the impact, readied to push him away, but he slammed into my bad shoulder. I hissed with the stabbing pain as his bulk unbalanced me and he sneered, looking to Green Tie for approval.

Green Tie, rushing forward, found DC Myers already vaulting over the reception desk. Asserting his police officer status made no difference as feet and fists scythed the air. Blue's eye blacked itself on my fist. Out of the corner of my eye, I spotted Cryptic Mascara woman swinging her handbag at my friend's head until a flying leg toppled her. Green Tie grunted as she landed on him, and Gaudy Woman's bright dress flashed in my vision. Nice, I thought, maliciously, as Brad gave Blue a breath-stealing thump. Blue's nose hit the marble deck with a crunch like a walnut being shelled.

I rolled clear of the seething bodies. Sharan pulled Gaudy Woman off the tangled pile. The woman shrieked, 'I'm calling the police!'

'I am the bloody police,' Sharan yelled. She retrieved her identity wallet from the floor.

Holmes, glaring at Blue, hauled him to his feet and pushed him away.

Myers, at the same time, tugged Green Tie to his feet and shoved him to the desk.

'You two,' Sharan got in Green's face, 'calm your tits, both of you. DC Myers, take statements.' He nodded and replied, 'Yes, ma'am.' 'Brad, can you drive me to Leon's hotel? The boss is on her way.'

I rubbed my sore shoulder. When I looked up, I found Blue Goon, blood staining his shirt and disgruntled face, giving me the evil eye like a misshapen Cyclops. One evil eye. His left eye was swollen shut while the right one threw daggers at me.

'John.' Holmes nudged my good elbow. 'Are you all right?'

'Yeah, fine. It's nothing.'

'I'm going to Anita's hotel.'

'We are,' I corrected him.

The drizzle had become a torrential downpour. Proper March rain bounced up from the puddled pavement. A cruising taxi pulled in at the sight of customers. We buckled up and sat in silence with our own thoughts. The windscreen wipers battling the Niagara cascading down the glass squeaked and scraped. I shuddered at the sound of the water clock counting the last minutes of Anita's life.

'You handled that well,' said Holmes.

'You weren't so bad yourself.' I smiled.

Twenty minutes later, after some poor learner driver got it in the neck for daring to stall at traffic lights, Anita's budget hotel presented a clean face to the street and a deserted desk to us. I tapped the portable brass bell on the counter. The neat, dark-haired receptionist appeared, reading slowly, her finger moving over the page as she walked. Closing the book, she stowed it out of sight and treated us to a natural friendly smile.

'A friend is staying here. Could you ring her room to fetch her down, please?' Holmes asked.

'No phone in room,' she answered in an Eastern European accent. 'Who is your friend?' He told her and gave our names. 'She is not in room when girl took towel up. You leave message, I tell her you came.'

'No, thank you. Do you know where she went?'

'I am sorry. Not seen her.'

'Thank you,' Holmes and I said together.

Holmes broke into a run on the pavement. We weaved through the revelers leaving the watering holes for their next stopovers. Holmes took a left at the end of the road. He kept up the blistering pace to the great edifice of Holborn Station.

'Where we going?' I asked, panting, a hand on the bright crimson news-stand.

'Bow Creek Marina. Anita's houseboat.'

We clattered down to the platform, hopped on the train, and sat in silence amid the throng of travelers. All observed the unwritten rule of not making eye contact with a stranger. Except for Holmes. His eyes roved from one passenger to the next, deducing the living daylights out of them. About forty overheated minutes later we emerged from the tunnel of the strictly functional Bromley-by-Bow Station. The rain had ceased, so that was a blessing.

'This way,' Holmes said.

We raced over soggy grass then took a short-cut between blocks of shoe-box flats to an industrial landscape. Further on, below the road bridge, a lonely lamp shed its sodium glow on a path beside a water channel. We trotted down wooden steps onto the poorly lit towpath. Grey modern warehouses loomed to our left, and neatly spaced trees flanked the river on our right.

About a mile on, Bow Creek Residential Marina, its sign freshly painted, snuggled against the broad sweep of the River Lea. Grassy parkland dotted with trees and bushes lay on the other side.

We skulked in the cover of the trees with a good view of the houseboats tied up beside a pontoon and along the stone-walled bank.

All the dozen vessels were unique in colour, size, and shape. Wisps of smoke rose lazily from narrow chimneys, and warm lights glowed from portholes. Water playfully slapped the hulls in the otherwise silent night.

'Anita's is "The Gloria Scott," the blue one with the tall wheelhouse.' Holmes whispered.

I shifted quietly to see better past the glossy leaves of a squat holly bush. "The Gloria Scott" stretching some fifty feet, though only about six or seven feet wide, was easy to identify. Her varnished wood wheelhouse jutted from her broad stern. Light shone from her windows and open doors. I glanced over my shoulder at a patter of feet behind us. I wondered how large the rats were until the hairy owner of the paws waggled its Spaniel backside and tail at us.

'Go away, doggy, go back to your owner. Shoo,' I said.

'You may as well just call it to you,' Holmes said, amused. He threw out his long arm to wave our fluffy visitor away. Furry-features promptly looked up into the dark sky and spun in circles, eagerly searching for whatever the nice man must have thrown for it to retrieve.

'That worked,' I said.

Holmes shot me a look of exasperated suffering.

'Tansy,' called a quiet female voice followed by stealthy footsteps. 'Tansy. Here,' she said more firmly.

Tansy whimpered, scampered away, and reappeared as quickly. Anita followed her and squeaked with alarm. Her hand, pale in the dim light, went to her heart.

'Oh, don't do that,' she exclaimed, stooping and running to join us. 'Someone came to the hotel, Mr. Holmes. A man. I thought it was you, so I went to the door. He said my dog was out loose. I told him to wait until I got my phone and purse. He was gross. He stank like something had died in his pocket.'

'Aha,' Holmes said as if it was important. 'Big, ugly?'

'Average, but I didn't like the look of him, so I rang my friend, Dee. She said it must be a stray. Tansy was laid on her rug in front of the fire with a chewy stick.'

'You used your phone?'

'No, you told me not to, so I borrowed Dee's and rang her land-line.'

'Good. Have you been back to your boat? The lights are on.'

'No way. Tansy needed a run and there was a lost dog, so I came by to check from a distance, but I didn't go aboard. He's there, Leon, isn't he?

'Unless it's your mystery visitor. What happened to him?'

'I don't know. I climbed out of the window.'

'Down a knotted sheet?' I asked, horrified.

'Just onto a flat roof with a fire escape. It wasn't too bad really. Not when there's a suspicious man leering at the door.'

Holmes produced his phone from his pocket, prised open its engraved custom metal cover, and began typing furiously. He ended with a triumphant look and a stab on the 'send' key.

'I've updated the police,' he said. 'Lestrade will be here soon. It's probably only Leon on the boat, John, if you'd like to come with me?'

'Yeah, I want to see this through to the end.'

Holmes broke cover, moving quietly toward "The Gloria Scott." I crept along with him.

'Wait! I want to see his face when you arrest him,' said Anita, calling Tansy to heel, scurrying to join us before Holmes could respond.

Tansy, refusing to go anywhere near the boat, froze and barked. We all instinctively stopped. Nice tableau. In the open, Tansy alerting the boat's occupant. Perfect. The reluctant Spaniel redoubled her effort to rouse the whole neighbourhood.

'Down. Get down,' Holmes shouted, yanking at Anita's wrist.

As one, Holmes, Anita and I, dropped face down onto the wet, muddy grass, Anita seizing Tansy.

The night ripped apart like tearing velvet. Black smoke and a gout of flame erupted from the wheelhouse doors.

'My home!' Anita cried out. Tansy licked her muddied face.

A male voice screamed, almost drowning out Anita's voice. The figure staggered from the wheelhouse, his arms windmilling. He fell onto the deck and blindly plunged headlong into the water. The second explosion blew out the windows, sending glass daggers flying through the air. Scraps of blazing wood whizzed, cartwheeling through the roiling, acrid mirk. A deathly silence fell.

'No, no, no,' Holmes growled.

Surefooted, he sprinted for the pontoon. My gammy leg failed me, I slipped in the mud and fell on my knees. My friend tore off his coat and flung it down on the boarding before diving into the ice-cold river. When I reached the spot Holmes had gone in, I saw nothing but charred debris bobbing on the black water.

'Sherlock!'

The splash guided my eyes to the surfacing head and arms. Holmes had the man in his grasp. I lay down and leaned out, straining to catch my friend's hand. Together we pushed and hauled the limp, heavy weight out of the clawing water. I dragged the man onto the boards. Holmes heaved himself onto the pontoon and sat with his knees to his chest, catching his breath.

'It's Steffan Leon,' he said, shivering violently in the chilly air.

I felt the comatose Leon for a pulse

'Shock and hypothermia,' I diagnosed, shaking my head. 'Sorry.' I fully expected to record the time of death in a minute or two.

I was bent over Leon, my fingers pinching his nose and my other hand holding his jaw, doing what little I could to keep him breathing until an ambulance arrived, when Holmes pressed his hand on my shoulder and murmured in Latin. The strangest sensation crept over me. I gained an impression of pipe smoke, turning wheels and a distant horse trotting on cobbles,

I inhaled sharply and rocked back on my heels, startled at Leon's eyelids suddenly flying open. He spluttered, moaned and, unsuccessfully, tried to sit up. I rolled him onto his side while trying to shake off the strange feeling induced by my friend's hand on my shoulder until distracted by the sound of feet thudding on the pontoon.

Anita, her arms pumping, stood out in silhouette, lit by the headlights of a paramedic's motorcycle bouncing across the park. He rode along the pontoon, passing her, and propped his machine on its side-stand. Anita ran up to us while we made way for the medic to work.

'Come on, you need dry clothes and something sweet and warm,' Anita told us, shaking with adrenaline and the cold.
She waved a hand at her neighbours flocking to give out tea and blankets. Revolving blue lights presaged the arrival of the police, and the Fire Service, red, urgent, and noisy, beat the ambulance to an invisible finish line.

Holmes accepted cargo pants and a sweater from Anita's tallest neighbour and changed in the snug warm cabin of a narrowboat. I surveyed the owner's collection of tin mugs decorated with improbably-painted flowers then passed one, containing hot chocolate, with miniature marshmallows floating on the surface, over to my friend.

He placed it on the table.

'Leon owes me a new phone,' he said, delving in his coat pocket for his metal case.

'It got wet.'

'No, it was in my coat pocket.' He opened the case and showed me the innards. A crack split the screen, and a whiff of something singed remained. 'That's a drawback of using magic, it kills technology unless it's shielded. It fried. Magic obeys Newton's Third Law.'

'Magic. It's been a hell of a day. I'm not really in the mood for one of your jokes, mate, tomorrow, yes, not right now.'

'I've no idea why you think I'm joking. I told you this morning. The effect of the Mossgrave Ritual was that I acquired a little ability. Magical ability. What did you think I was doing back there, giving Leon absolution?'

'Using magic cracked your phone screen and fried it? If you are having me on, Sherlock, I'm going to rip your arm off and beat you to death with the soggy end.'

'Leon was on the point of shuffling off this mortal coil, you said so yourself then he was fine and dandy and trying to sit up. You're an excellent doctor, but you must agree that something you cannot explain with science occurred when I had my hand on your shoulder.'

A strangled laugh in the air was mine. 'That Latin you said, that was…a magic spell? That's just bonkers.'

'And my phone just blew itself apart and smells like incinerated plastic. Using magic can fry brains too, if used without caution.'

My cup almost visited my lap. 'You did a Harry Potter on Leon.'

'A who?' John, you're going to spill your hot chocolate.'

'Bloody hell,' I said, righting my cup. 'Your brain, Sherlock. Look, I know how much it means to you to solve challenging cases, but as your friend and a doctor, I have to tell you it can't be worth that price.'

'I owed Trev. I owed his father for convincing me that my amusing, worthless hobby had a practical use. Don't fret, I use magic sparingly.'

'But you didn't even touch Leon.'

'I didn't need to. You were working on him, not me. I just cast an enhancer spell that gave you a little boost.' Holmes looked a tad like he had just realised he'd overstepped the mark. 'It was only a very small spell, I didn't think you'd mind,' he said, drawing back, shielding himself with his drink.

'You're incredible.' I said, my voice emerging hoarser than a raven's croak after it had spent the night swigging whisky and smoking fat cigars. Sorry, I digress, the dissolute raven is another case for another time.

'Thank you. You are a good friend. My only friend, in fact.'

'Charming,' said a female voice from the steps to the deck.

'DI Lestrade.' Holmes chimed. 'We are frolleagues. Friendly colleagues.'

'Like I said, charming. Brad's here to drive you home. I'll send Sharan around for your statements in the morning. Just omit the unmentionable, and we'll be good to go.'

'Does Lestrade know about you having magical ability?' I asked in a whisper as Holmes and I made our weary way to Brad's car.

'Yes, she officially works on cases with a suspected magical component but the Met, the Fae and the government alike prefer to keep it all a secret. Imagine what chaos there'd be if the whole world was aware of the existence of unicorns, Fae, fairies, and shape-shifting witches. Don't mention any of that in Brad's hearing, he doesn't know.'

Brad duly took us back to Baker Street, in his posh car, in companionable silence.

I poured Holmes and myself whisky and soda at Baker Street before I was ready to mention the unmentionable.

'The enhancer spell that helped me retrieve Leon from death's door? Any long-term effects on me?' I asked.

'Sorry, that was a temporary fix.'

'No, that's reassuring, actually.'

'Fair enough. Anything else?'

'While you were casting the spell... I can't describe it. Like I had an idea of hooves on stone cobbles and pipe smoke.'

Holmes nodded. 'It's called a trace, from Old French. It's like a person's handwriting, individual to human practitioners of magic. A trace of a spell. It must be your Scottish ancestry; most people don't notice it. It can be masked, but it uses a lot of energy to do so. Hoxley did that.'

'You'd have known straight away if Hoxley hadn't hidden her trace?'

'I would. That's why she cast a glamour with added oomph. Silly woman, she knew the risks. Using that much energy continuously will have cost her dearly. I was surprised she combusted the boat.'

'What is she? A witch or a fairy. Or something else?'

'Part Fae, part mortal human. A witch is near enough. They're not all like that, she's just a bad example.' He paused. 'John, you look done in. It's late.'

That was an understatement. I sloped off to bed.

Lestrade herself, called in to Baker Street the following morning with news. Hoxley, looking her true age without her glamour spell enhancing her voice and beauty, had been caught at the airport. DC Myers had arrested the two goons from the hotel for obstructing the police in the course of their duty and, she informed us, their employer was also a victim of Hoxley and Leon.

'Ah,' said Holmes, not lifting his head from his experiment with one of his home-made wine recipes. A chemistry experiment I encourage rather than those that result in noxious fumes.

Lestrade winked at me. 'Mr. Leon's refusing to answer questions until you visit him. He's got 'no comment' on repeat play. He wants to speak to you.'

'My blushes,' Holmes said. And yawned.

'He's asked for John.'

Half the tub of yeast he was playing with dropped into the glass dish.

'Why me? I mean, I'll go if it'll help,' I said.

Lestrade shrugged her shoulders. 'I'm just telling you Leon's refusing to help us wrap up the case. He's a jittering mess. I think he's terrified Sherlock will take his revenge on him for conning his father's friend. Leon's a criminal, and you're a doctor not, if you'll pardon me saying this, you're not a detective or a mage. Doctors save people.'

'Doctors are the worst when they go wrong,' Holmes remarked.

I laughed. 'Sherlock saved him, not me.'

'He was out of it when I weaved the enhancer. In his eyes, you saved his life,' he said.

'I'll give you a ride to Bart's?' she offered.

Half an hour later, Holmes and I stood at Leon's bedside. The confident charmer had dissolved into a frightened little man who shrank into his blankets at the sight of Holmes.

'I know what Hoxley did and I know what you've done,' said Holmes. 'I'll tell you, and if I'm wrong on any point you can shout up.' Leon nodded enough to loosen his head. 'She had you enchanted. Under her spell.'

Leon croaked and pulled the cover to his chin. He looked frantically at me as if expecting to be fully turned into a frog.

'Hoxley was jealous about you spending time with Anita. She could feel she was losing her hold on you, so you played up to her in the restaurant trying to convince her that she could count on you, that Anita meant nothing to you.'

Leon nodded, scrunching the blanket in his fists as if it were a talisman.

'That tacky nightclub – you were surrounding yourself with people for safety from her. I surmise she divined that you were lying to her, so she sent a draugr to Anita's hotel. Hoxley intended her to be murdered, and she would have been if the clever girl hadn't escaped.'

'Anita's good and kind. I l-love her,' Leon stammered.

'You put her life at risk, twice!' I exclaimed. 'What were you going to do next, go on the run from the wicked witch of the West End?' I shook my head. 'Unbelievable.'

Holmes continued, calm and clinical as before, 'Hoxley decided to silence you both permanently and blew up the boat. The only good news I have for you is she was arrested by DI Lestrade attempting to leave the country. On a plane. I believe the excessive use of magic needed to maintain her glamour, summon a draugr, give it an appearance less like one of the Undead, command it and also explode Anita's home from a distance sapped her powers to a critical level.'

'That means she can't harm me now? Am I safe from her? Please, if you know you must tell me,' Leon, the picture of desperation, mewled.

'She hasn't frazzled the entire contents of her brain attic, but she's certainly doomed to spend the rest of her life in a Fae prison where she won't be able to practice magic. I dare say you will also stand before a Fae jury. The Fae take an exceedingly dim view of endangering the life of a mortal human. Enjoy hospital food while you can.'

A crime against humanity, literally. No wonder Steffan Leon was too busy sweating and trembling to thank Holmes for saving his life before we left. We marched out of the arch at Bart's being overlooked by the only surviving statue of Henry VIII in London, his feet planted apart, airing his crown jewels in the sunshine. I glanced up at the niche. 'I think we need to talk about all this witchery-woo stuff.'

Holmes grinned. 'Lunch in a Fae place I know?'

'Not today.'

The cheer dropped off his face. 'As you wish.'

'Mm, no. I was looking at the clock. I was thinking that we'd better get back to Baker Street, and you can tell me all about this mage-malarkey after this morning's appointment. Letter stapled to the mantelpiece?'

'Crumbs, is it Tuesday?'

'All day.' I grinned.

Cue a taxi appearing as if by magic. It must have been a Fae driver since he didn't spontaneously combust when Holmes mentioned the draugr, but he did peek nervously at us in his driving mirror.

The morning newspaper carried a believable story about the reluctant Spaniel who saved her owner's life seconds before petrol fumes ignited and caused her houseboat to blow up. One line had been given to an anonymous female witness assisting the police in an alleged fraud case.

'Gloria made the news,' I said, pointing out the honourable mention.

'Gloria who?' Holmes zoomed in for a look.

'Your tarty waitress and night-clubbing persona. Gloria Scott.'

Holmes laughed, a deep hearty rumble. 'You are quite bonkers. And a dreadful flat-mate. By the way, who's Harry Potter?'

'Yeah. Coming to that. Your turn to make the tea first.'

All Roads Lead to Holmes

All Roads Lead to Holmes by Trudence Holtz

Sherlock: The Abominable Episode
By Margaret Walsh

When the BBC announced that there was going to be a special episode of their hit show "Sherlock" the internet went into meltdown. Photos turned up of various cast members dressed in Victorian costumes, and the excitement and interest levels skyrocketed. When the time came for its release, both in the cinema and on TV, the expectations were high. Perhaps too high. Sherlock: The Abominable Bride became the Marmite of television. You either loved the episode, or you hated it. There were no half measures. Let's take a look at the episode. (If you haven't seen the episode, you may wish to skip over this essay.) There will be spoilers.

It started off well with an opening montage of scenes from the first three series, then a clock ticking back to the 19th century. Nicely done and made so that someone who was drawn to it for the Victorian content could get the context for the actual series. There were some nice touches, Speedy's café becoming Speedwell's Restaurant and Tearooms, for example.

The Victorian opening sequences were excellent. Sir Arthur Conan Doyle's "A Study in Scarlet" narration by Watson explaining how he came to be in London was used verbatim in a voice-over by Martin Freeman. The meeting with Stamford at the Criterion Hotel was there, and Sherlock Holmes beating a corpse with a stick. Elegant and slick.

The sequence that set the stage for the plot has Holmes and Watson returning to Baker Street. It bore a great deal of resemblance to a similar sequence in "The Private Life of Sherlock Holmes," a film that is close to the hearts of both Sherlock writers, Steven Moffat and Mark Gatiss.

It is at this point that things begin to go a little weird. As the pivot, Moffat and Gatiss use the untold ACD story of Ricoletti and his abominable wife. The wife being the bride of the episode title. The bride shoots herself but then is seen murdering her husband in Limehouse and then appears to go on a killing spree, murdering extremely unpleasant men.

Moffat and Gatiss begin to give the viewer hints that all may not be what it seems. The first one comes in the morgue scene with Sherlock saying of the bride: "How could he survive?" Instead of "How could she survive." A reference to Moriarty, who at the end of season two blew his brains out on the roof of Bart's and made a mysterious reappearance at the end of the last episode of season three. This is the first inkling we have that this is not going to be a simple Victorian murder mystery.

The scene in the glasshouse at night as Holmes and Watson wait for the bride to strike sets the tone. Watson suddenly becomes extremely nosy about Holmes's past. Asking: 'What made you like this?' Eliciting the response: 'Oh Watson. Nothing made me. I made me.' An odd exchange made even odder by the fact that when Watson mentions Holmes has a photo of Irene Adler inside his watch, we see the photo, and it is 21st century Irene!

If we watch carefully from the beginning, it does become obvious that Holmes is a caricature. He is too rude, too abrupt, and too dismissive to be a proper portrayal of Sir Arthur Conan Doyle's creation. He is, however, quite possibly how Sherlock views himself within the confines of his own mind. When we realize that we can see how the other characters are simply constructs of Sherlock's currently drug-addled mind.

It hits home hardest when we see Mycroft – a character who bears more resemblance to Mr. Creosote in "Monty Python's Meaning of Life" than he does to the man described in "The Bruce-Partington Plans" as having '…the tidiest and most orderly brain, with the greatest capacity for storing facts, of any man living.' Mark Gatiss' Mycroft in this episode is storing fat rather than facts. The whole bet between Mycroft and Sherlock on when Mycroft will die is quite revolting.

That the events are occurring within Sherlock's mind becomes clearer when Mycroft uses the phrases "crime scene" and "virus in the data." Not phrases that were in the vocabularies of 19th-century gentlemen, no matter how intelligent they were. Just in case we haven't got the message, a visit to Baker Street by the dead Moriarty shakes Sherlock out of his drugged state of mind and back into the 21st century. Sherlock explains he is using the unsolved case of Emelia Ricoletti (AKA the Abominable Bride) to work out how Moriarty has come back from the dead.

We realize that Sherlock is sliding in and out of reality when he and Lestrade, watched by Mycroft, exhume the corpse of

Emelia Ricoletti, which then comes to life, in a scene which had an entire cinema of viewers screaming their lungs out. Gothic horror at its finest.

The story works well on paper, but is far too self-indulgent in places. The scene at the Diogenes Club conducted in sign language was both unnecessary and cringe invoking. The scene felt like it had been dropped into the plot by the writers because they found it funny, even though it does nothing to drive the narrative forward. The humour is school-boyish, and I could envisage Mark Gatiss and Steven Moffat sniggering as they wrote it. The concierge at the Diogenes Club being called Wilder was a nice tip of the hat to "The Private Life of Sherlock Holmes" director, but ultimately did nothing to make that scene actually watchable or enjoyable.

There are some nice touches for the avid Sherlock Holmes fan. The opening Victorian narration, as I mentioned, but there were many others. I won't mention all of them, but they include the five orange pips sent to one victim of the bride before his death, and the reconstruction of several Paget illustrations, most notably Reichenbach Falls. The stained -glass in the door of 221 Baker Street is a replica of the cover of the first edition of the 'Hound of the Baskervilles'. And, of course, Sherlock delivers the immortal, though non-Canonical, line: "Elementary, my dear Watson."

The Reichenbach Fall scene is well-conceived. Holmes literally wrestles with his demons in the form of Moriarty, who taunts Holmes, "Not in your mind. I'll never be dead there." A trenchant observation. The arrival of Watson to save the day shows the trust Sherlock has in John. He knows that whatever happens, John will be there for him. They are a unit. When Moriarty complains, "That's not fair. There are two of you." John replies calmly, "There's always two of us," before booting Moriarty over the falls.

Though the main thrust of the plot is Holmes dealing with his demons, the bride's story is one of women. Unseen, unregarded, the enemy in a war that the male of the species must lose. This subplot, however, felt like it had been crammed in to simply bulk out the show. Nothing was really resolved, and it mostly felt flat. Even Mary Morstan working for Mycroft didn't have the power punch of surprise that you would expect.

The final scene in Victorian Baker Street is a nice touch. We are left wondering just which version of Sherlock Holmes was doing the dreaming. This becomes especially obvious when Holmes says, "I've always known I was a man out of his time" as he walks to the window and looks out onto a Victorian Baker Street vista, which morphs into the 21st-century one.

"Sherlock: The Abominable" was a good film, though it feels both rushed and crushed. Rushed in that you get the feeling it was a case of getting something out before the fans forget us, and crushed with the weight of unnecessary scenes and padding. While it is frustrating to know that this could have been a great film, if a little more care had been taken, it remains a good film and should be appreciated as such.

Hand Holding by Thinkanddoodle

Sherloccoli "The Broccoli" Holmes
By Paul Thomas Miller

The Baker Street Genius of the Brassica Genus
Being A Reprint From Patient Records
of John "Doctor" Watson

"I am inclined to think-" said I.

Sherloccoli Holmes did not answer, because he is a head of broccoli. I tried again; "I AM INCLINED TO THINK-"

I believe that I am one of the most long-suffering of mortals; but I'll admit that I was annoyed at the lack of clever interruption. Indeed, nothing came from the consulting legume other than an eyeless glare and a green silence.

Before I could question Sherloccoli on the reason for his taciturnity, the door of our apartment swung open. No sooner had Billy the pageboy announced Inspector Old MacDonald than the man himself marched into the room. He loomed over us. I found his six-foot of height so imposing I had to ask him to step down from the table and use the floor like the rest of us.

"I apologise for the intrusion, gentlemen," he began, "but I have encountered a case so baffling I don't know where to start. The ticket inspector of the Clapham omnibus has vanished from the top floor of his bus, leaving only his socks standing in his place."

We both looked expectantly at Holmes, but as he barely flinched, it was left to me to ask Old MacDonald to continue his narrative. "Continue your narrative," I said. "Edward Futon is a ticket inspector upon the London omnibuses. This morning, at half-past ten, he boarded the Clapham omnibus. It seems he went to make his way to the top deck of the bus.

The driver stopped him and told him that there was no one on the upper deck. "I shall be the judge of that," he told the driver, in an unusually brusque manner." "The driver, Charles O'Cheddary, says that such rudeness was quite uncharacteristic of the ticket inspector. When Futon had not come down from the top deck twenty minutes later, O'Cheddary stopped the bus at Clapham Common and went to investigate. The scene on the top deck was quite beyond his comprehension. Edward Futon had completely vanished. In his place, a pair of woolen socks stood upright on the floor in a small pool of blood. O'Cheddary can testify that the socks are those of Futon, being of a particular shade of grey. The blood, however, he claims not to have seen before."

Sherloccoli remained silent. So as not to embarrass the inspector, I elected to pretend Sherloccoli was talking. I surreptitiously wobbled him, concealed my mouth, and did my best impression of talking broccoli. "What size shoe does O'Cheddary take?" he appeared to ask in a falsetto Welsh accent.

"I have no idea, Mr. Holmes."

"Then perhaps Watson and I should investigate the scene. We will meet you at the omnibus at six this evening."

I was walking the inspector to the door when he peered over my shoulder and called to Sherloccoli, "Do you have any advice to give me in the meantime, Mr. Holmes?"

Naturally, Holmes did not reply because he is some broccoli. Nevertheless, I imagined him giving an answer of some description, and then I slammed the door in the inspector's face.

When I had finished crying, I asked Sherloccoli what he intended to do next. "It is quite the three pipe problem," I imagined Sherloccoli saying. So I jabbed three pipes in his stem, lit them, and retired to a safe distance.

When we met Old MacDonald at the omnibus that evening, Holmes was feeling weary, so I carried him up to the top deck to examine the scene. Placing him on the floor, I addressed the inspector. "Holmes is quite tired," I explained, "He has been working on the solution to this problem all day." "And what did you discover Holmes?" the inspector asked him.

Unfortunately, I was having another episode, so Holmes was unable to reply. Because he is just some broccoli. Even if he had been able to speak, it is unlikely that anyone would have heard him over the sound of my sobbing. As Holmes rolled under one of the omnibus seats and back out into the small puddle of blood, I felt the world slipping away and fell into unconsciousness.

Sometime the following morning, I woke to find Sherloccoli Holmes singing me The Happy Song while dancing across my bed. In any other head of broccoli, I would have been surprised, but I had learned his ways long ago and simply smiled. And while Mrs. Hudson, the police and my unhappy wife all insist there is no such person as Inspector Old MacDonald and that Sherloccoli Holmes is nothing but a vegetable, I am proud to add the Adventure of the Clapham Omnibusman to the many hundreds of cases which Sherloccoli and I failed to solve.

A Trio of Poems
By Toti

While English is not her first language Toti wrote the following three poems as a reaction to the BBC Sherlock television series. She explains her motivation:

"I needed to write these poems because in some way I felt that I was feeling what Sherlock felt. I always made them at his point of view. I just wrote what they make me feel. Sherlock is not a romantic but he has feelings like everyone else. I loved to think that I could speak about what was on his heart but not on his mouth."

The poems express the importance that Benedict Cumberbatch's Sherlock had for many people all over the world, and how it brought new perspective into the Sherlockian community.

Dear John Watson,
What did I do wrong?
My dear John Watson,
I promised you you weren't alone.

My dear best friend,
I swear I took care of her.
You do not know how I regret.
Maybe I should have taken her place.

My dear family,
Why do I feel you are so far?
If I'm high or if I die
Nothing matters if you're not by my side.

My dear John Watson,
I'd go to hell just to make you smile.
Just to make you rise, believe me,
I'm sure that I would die.

Dear John,

I've always been a ridiculous man.
Suddenly my hope is only an ash.
We run together, you save my ass.
I solve murders and you save lives.

If I told you what scares me
Would you run away?
My head denies and denies,
You said "I am not gay."

But if I told you what happens to me,
Perhaps, will it change?
If I told you I fell for you,
I don't want to see the end.

Now I'm alone and you are married.
This is the game and I am tired.
I looked for love and now you find it -
Your happiness is my happiness.
So let's go - I wanna see you flying.

Why does it seem so impossible?
That love so catastrophical.
I let you down, I'm not a hero,
Not an angel, not in the middle.

Maybe I don't care
What everybody feels,
But I really care
If you are not here.

Take my hand
And show me the way.
I need to talk.
Sherlock is a girl's name.

I look sad when you can't see.
Now you are the owner of my breath.
For me, it's hard to talk about what I feel
But now I need to say
I love you. And have always been like this.

A Limerick
By Bob Madia

Of Sherlock Holmes I've always been a fan-a
He'll always be the 'best and wisest man'-a
Be it movie or book
I'll always take a look
I even named my daughter Sherlocki-Anna

The Watsons At Home
By Wanda Dow

The young marrieds sat in front of the fireplace as was their habit every evening before dinner. The husband, a doctor by trade, was fidgeting with his pipe as the wife read through the final pages of a stack of papers in her lap.

Mary turned the last page of the manuscript over, a hint of a smile on her lips. She looked over at her husband, the author, trying to nonchalantly light his pipe as he awaited her reaction.

"Well now," she finally spoke, her voice barely audible over the crackling fire. "You've certainly written a fine novel, John. It's been very interesting to me to read what went on when I wasn't there. And you've made it all so entertaining. Do you intend to try to sell it as you did the other?"

"Only with your permission, my dear," replied the husband. "It is, after all, your story, Mary."

"Mm," she nodded, ironing the pages with her hand.

"If you do not wish me to pursue publication," he stated adamantly, "Just say the word. I would never have anything printed without permission. And I would certainly not wish to cause you any harm, my dear."

She leaned forward and placed the manuscript into his lap, then rested back in her wing chair. "Dear, sweet John. I must say that I certainly gained more by losing a chest full of pearls than anyone will ever know."

For the first time, John seemed to relax.

"Then the story did not upset you?"

"Well," she pondered that thought for a moment before speaking. "I do have to admit that your first description of me was not all that complimentary."

His mouth opened to protest, but she held up her hand to stop him.

"However, your statement after I left made up for it." She tilted her head slightly, as if viewing her husband from a different angle would ensure the truth. "Did you truly say 'what a very attractive woman'?"

He took her hand and stared into her large blue eyes, "Upon my honor, madame, I did."

She laughed in delight at his serious expression and took her hand from his grasp so that she could wag a finger at him.

"And there is one thing you have written in error, my love!" She frowned in mock disapproval.

He spread his arms wide, "Tell me and I shall correct whatever has caused your disfavor."

"You told Mr. Sherlock Holmes that you feared that it was the last investigation that you would have the chance of studying."

"Yes," he stated, "And rightly so. I am a married man now. I have responsibilities. I cannot go traipsing about the city in search of villains and hoodlums. I learned quickly that it can be a very dangerous game that my friend plays. What would become of my family should something happen to its provider?"

"Although it would grieve your family greatly should you suffer any harm," Mary stated with a wry smile, "it would get along as it did before. Don't you dare use me as an excuse to not assist Mr. Holmes should he request it."

"All right then," he said, straightening his shoulders, "But what of my medical practice?"

"Barely begun," she stated. "And we've neighbors who are qualified to take over for a few days absence. Besides, what you really love is the writing. I can see it in your face when you're working at your desk. I can tell it by your demeanor. Oh, I know you enjoy your medical practice, too, but once you'd finished this, you were lost. It was as if nothing else could hold your interest. You were restless."

He nodded. "I shall take what you have said into consideration, madame."

She studied his face for a moment before reaching for her needlepoint. "Good," said she.

They sat in silence then, she with her needle and thread, he with his pipe and manuscript.

"But I must beg to differ with you concerning that what I really love is writing," he spoke up, surprising her.

"Oh?" she asked, ready to begin again her argument that they would get by no matter what their financial status.

His eyes crinkled ever so slightly as he tried to suppress a smile, "What I truly love, Mrs. Watson, is you!"

So You Want to Write…
By Robert Perret

SO YOU WANT TO WRITE A
SHERLOCK HOLMES STORY

1. Holmes is engrossed in some diversion

2. Watson has your Accu-Weather forecast

3. A Knock at the door

4. A client with a crazy story

5. Holmes is like "aight I guess"

6. The police think they have it figured out but they don't.

7. Holmes calls their attention to something

8. Holmes then places an advert in the newspaper.

9. The villain confronts Holmes at Baker Street

10. Holmes + Watson wear disguises and lay in wait

11. The scoundrel is undone

12. Watson may or may not know what became of the client

FINIS

Holmes and Watson by Spacefall

The Twist of Sherlock Holmes
By Phil Attwell

I am Agatha Manders, and this is how I twisted the Great Sherlock Holmes and Doctor Watson, or, as I like to call them, Dearest Darling (DD for short) and Watto. I was the maid for Charles Augustus Milverton. Milly, as I called him once or twice when he paid me late. My cousin is Bunny Manders, who you may know, wrote about his exploits with AJ Raffles. I do have nick'em names for them too, but I'm not sure the world is ready for them.

You may recall how DD was out to get Milly 'cos of his evil blackmailing ways. To learn about the doings, goings, and mappings of Milly's Towers he thought to woo me and offer marriage to me.

Milly kept a big household staff, three maids beside me: Brenda Mannikin, Molly Mandy, and Boa Constricta. There was also a footman, a Batman, a handyman, a Butler called Billy. The Coachman doubled as a bodyguard, and we called him Russell Muscle, but not when he was listening.

Bunny & Raffles got me the job through contacts at the Northumberland Avenue Turkish Bath, and they have given me a list of documents they would like me to "borrow" from Milly. They were: Two papers relating to them:

A paper about Inspectors Lestrade and Mackenzie
The Turkish bath attendance list dated 4 November 1889
The 221b Baker Street rent book
And Watto's marriage certificate.

I was also warned that DD was on Milly's case. So I was not surprised when he turned up in one of his silly disguises, saying he was a plumber called Ballcock. He even did the down on his knees stuff. And he was a pretty good kisser.

Also, Inspector Lestrade approached me secretly to tell me he knew what DD was up to and wanted me to help, but he didn't think DD knew that he knew and that he would protect me from any fallout.

So the night arrived when DD & Watto came secretly to get some documents from the safe. The night before, Milly was drunk. I stole his keys and took the documents listed beforehand and kept them upon my personage.

DD wasn't any better a safecracker than he was a plumber, so it was taking him ages to open it. Just as he did, this pish-posh lady breaks in, has a set to with Milly, shoots him with a dead shot, and sets a fire upon the fancy curtains that DD & Watto were hiding behind.

So Pish-Posh Lady escapes, leaving me to appear and wink at DD & Watto and help them to burn the contents of the safe in the curtain conflagration. DD said he didn't want to risk the safe protecting them. Then I raised the alarm. Billy Butler and Russell Muscle chased DD and Watto over the nice stripy lawn before they could escape over the lowest part of the wall that I had told DD about during one of our smooches.

Milly was now dead, lots of people slept easier. But we all lost our jobs and home.

Lestrade was true to his word and got me a new billet as a maid for a retired opera singer who also knew something of DD. We would exchange our tales over wine and cheesy biscuits.

As for Raffles and Bunny, I gave them all the documents except the ones relating to them in the hope that I could persuade them to go straight. That was a bad plan as Bunny ended up in jail. Raffles kept faking his death until he did it for real in a South African battle that also wounded Bunny. Now Bunny is writing again, and I've been keeping those documents well hidden. Last night Bunny is got an award at a Freemason Hall in Whitechapel for his writing and work on prison reform.

Romance is in the air for me again now. Last night I walked out with Mr. Christie. I hope it goes somewhere this time. Maybe we'll get married and have a daughter. She won't have to go a-maiding like me. Me and Bunny will learn her how to write twists.

I just checked on the documents. They were missing. Maybe Raffles wasn't dead after all.

Detective Pikachu by iamjohnlocked4life

The Canonical Credentials of Detective Pikachu
By Paul Thomas Miller

(Spoiler alert: In stating my case, I must, by necessity, spoil the film for those who have not seen it. Some might say that the film is its own spoiler because it is dreadful, to which I would respond: "Sucks to be you, misery-guts")

It has been said that the 2019 movie Pokémon Detective Pikachu is not a Sherlock Holmes film. The naysayers would have us believe that the only link between Sherlock Holmes and Detective Pikachu is the deerstalker hat, which through erroneous association with Sherlock Holmes has come to be visual shorthand for "this character is a detective".

It is my contention, however, that Pokémon Detective Pikachu is the most Canonical film ever produced. My argument is based upon Monsignor Ronald A. Knox's 1911 paper: Studies in the Literature of Sherlock Holmes. For many, this paper constitutes the foundation of Holmesian Studies. Apart from the Canon itself, there can be no greater source material to work from. I am principally interested in the passage in which Knox describes the structure of Canonical stories:

"The actual scheme of each should consist... of eleven distinct parts; the order of them may in some cases be changed about, and more or less of them may appear as the story is closer to or further from the ideal type."

He goes on to describe the eleven parts as follows:

1. The Proömion, a homely Baker Street scene, with invaluable personal touches, and sometimes a demonstration by the detective.

2. Exegesis kata ton diokonta, that is, the client's statement of the case.

3. The Ichneusis, or personal investigation, often including the famous floor-walk on hands and knees.

4. The Anaskeue, or refutation on its own merits of the official theory of Scotland Yard.

5. The first Promenusis (exoterike) which gives a few stray hints to the police, which they never adopt.

6. The second Promenusis (esoterike), which adumbrates the

true course of the investigation to Watson alone. This is sometimes wrong, as in the 'Yellow Face'.

7. The Exetasis, or further following up of the trial, including the cross-questioning of relatives, dependents, etc., of the corpse (if there is one), visits to the Record Office, and various investigations in an assumed character.

8. The Anagnorisis, in which the criminal is caught or exposed.

9. The second Exegesis (kata ton pheugonta), that is to say the criminal's confession.

10. The Metamenusis, in which Holmes describes what his clues were and how he followed them.

11. The Epilogos, sometimes comprised in a single sentence. This conclusion often contains a gnome or quotation from some standard author.

He also explains that No. 1 and No. 11 are invariable, Nos. 2 and 3 are almost always present and Nos. 4, 5 and 6 are less necessary. He makes no comment on the necessity of Nos. 7 through 10.

I suggest that eponymous deerstalkered Pikachu represents Sherlock Holmes, Tim Goodman is our Dr. John H. Watson and Ryme City is our London. With this in mind, it is easy to demonstrate that Pokémon Detective Pikachu meets the Canonical criteria laid out by Knox.

1. The Proömion

While the film does open on a homely Leaventown scene in which Tim Goodman and his friend Jack are out for one last Pokémon hunting jaunt together, it is not really what Knox required of a Proömion. While Knox claims that a Proömion is an "invariable" component, it's apparent absence is not necessarily a problem. Knox states the stories which provide evidence for his eleven parts. Among them is A Study in Scarlet, which also lacks the "invariable" Proömion. Why? Because Holmes and Watson had not met yet. Similarly, in Pokémon Detective Pikachu Pikachu and Tim have not met yet.

Like Watson in A Study in Scarlet, this story starts with Tim, sad and lonely. Tim's own Murray-the-orderly (Jack) tries to save him (from stagnation rather than enemy bullets) before they part company. Tim is then told that his father, Harry Goodman, has died in the course of his duty as a Ryme City police officer. This is his life-changing moment tallying with Watson being injured out of the military – both events are unexpected game-changers. Soon after, he arrives in Ryme City with "neither kith nor kin [nor Pokémon]." Like Watson arriving in London, Tim is traumatised and devoid of purpose and direction at this point. It is in his subsequent meeting with Pikachu that his life takes a turn for the better. Thus, Pokémon Detective Pikachu starts with a perfectly Canonical Study in Scarlet style Proömion.

2. Exegesis kata ton diokonta

There are two contenders for the "statement of the case." The first is in Tim's encounter with Lucy Stevens at Harry Goodman's apartment (13 minutes in). Here she intimates that Harry was murdered because he was working on something important. However, this is not so much a statement of a case as it is a suggestion of a case.

A more obvious statement comes when Tim and Pikachu first meet at 18 minutes in. Pikachu categorically states that something is amiss, that he is investigating and that Tim should assist him. This is our proper Exegesis kata ton diokonta.

3. The Ichneusis

At 18 minutes in, Tim discovers Pikachu creeping around on the floor, investigating Harry's apartment. The palpable Ichneusis is, then, Tim and Pikachu's very first meeting, although there are arguably others to be found in the film, such as the investigation at the PCL Facility.

4. The Anaskeue

At 24 minutes in Pikachu is attempting to convince Tim that they need to find Harry. Tim believes this is impossible, because the police say Harry died. Pikachu denies this. He points out that just because the police believe something, it does not mean it is true. He refutes the official theory thus:

"Did they find a body? No, I didn't think so. And by the way, did that report also say that I'm dead?"

The Anaskeue, then, is clearly present.

5. The first Promenusis

This comes at 43 minutes in. After being arrested at The Roundhouse, Tim tells Lieutenant Hide Yoshida about the experimental Pokémon drug "R" and that Harry may still be alive. Yoshida does not believe him. True to the first Promenusis structure, Tim and Pikachu have given the police some valuable hints which they ignore.

6. The second Promenusis

There are several examples of second Promenusis in Pokémon Detective Pikachu, and this is for an important plot reason. Pikachu represents a Sherlock Holmes who has temporarily gone wrong. While he is put right at the end of the film, throughout the main story he is battling to recover his deductive abilities. For this reason, his theories develop and change as he gains more clues and evidence. I can identify at least three "second" Promenusis.

At 28 minutes, Pikachu shares his clues and thoughts with Tim for the first time.

At 48 minutes, after meeting Howard Clifford, Tim and Pikachu revise their theory and are somewhat misdirected (representing a lazy mistake comparable to the one in The Yellow Face).

At 59 minutes, as they investigate the PCL Facility, Pikachu shares his theories with Tim as he forms them.

7. The Exetasis

This Exetasis of this film is very similar to one of the longer Canonical stories e.g. A Study in Scarlet, The Sign of the Four or The Valley of Fear. In those stories (at least in the Holmes and Watson sections), a lot of the writing is about the investigation itself. Detective Pikachu is no different, and the majority of the film is comprised of the Exetasis.

At 32 minutes, they follow up the "R" clue with Lucy Stevens, who provides them with further information.

At 35 minutes, they interrogate Mr. Mime.

At 55 minutes, they investigate the PCL Facility. It is worth noting that they do this by illegally breaking into the premises – a typically Holmesian technique, as seen when he breaks into the home of Charles Augustus Milverton or when Watson deceives his way into the home of Baron Gruner.

At 70 minutes, an Exetasis leads to a second Promenusis when Mewtwo tries to tell Tim and Pikachu the real facts of the case but is interrupted. The limited information leads them to draw incorrect conclusions.

At 76 minutes, Pikachu discovers his vital clue at the scene of Harry's crash.

At 80 minutes, Pikachu discovers the last details by talking to Psyduck-Lucy.

8. The Anagnorisis

Here we see the narrative structure of the movie, by necessity, forcing the order of the parts to alter slightly. The Exegesis occurs before the Anagnorisis. Nevertheless, they are both present. Indeed both versions of the Anagnorisis are here; exposure and capture. First, there is exposure when Clifford makes a public announcement of his plans at 79 minutes. Then he is captured by Pikachu, Tim, and Psyduck-Lucy at 87 minutes.

9. Exegesis

While it could be said that the public announcement at 79 minutes is a form of Exegesis, the private confession of Mewtwo-Clifford to Tim at 77 minutes is a far more Canonical one.

10. Metamenusis

The place of the Metamenusis is somewhat distorted by the way Pikachu is updating Tim throughout the movie. As discussed earlier, this is due to the plot being about a "broken-Sherlock" trying to fix himself. However, a robust Metamenusis does exist at around 76 minutes. It is in the form of a soliloquy but it nevertheless sees Pikachu tying up loose ends to present a coherent solution to the mystery.

11. Epilogos

While it could be argued that the whole scene starting at 90 minutes (in which Harry and Pikachu meet with Tim and essentially agree to team up) could be taken as a long Epilogos, for my money Pikachu's final line really offers the kind of quotable conclusion Knox had in mind: "Pika, pika!"

As Knox suggests that "more or less [parts] may appear as the story is closer to or further from the ideal type", it is worthy of note that Detective Pikachu contains all 11 parts. It meets Knox's expectations to such a degree that it is a very Canonical movie. However, there are further points to consider which raise the film beyond merely being highly Canonical. I believe Knox missed several other factors that make a story Canonical.

A. Problematica

There are many problems in the Canon which Holmesians like to consider and which are highly characteristic. There is Watson's wandering wound, the incompatible dates of the Great Hiatus and Wisteria Lodge, John's wife calling him James and many others. Pokémon Detective Pikachu Canonically comes with its own problematica. For example: Tim manages to go the whole film without recognising his dad's voice and at one point Pikachu on foot (and tiny legs) manages to walk from the PCL Facility back to Ryme City almost as quickly as Tim and Lucy drive there. As in the Canon, these are subtle, inconsequential errors which do nothing to ruin the story but provide material for potential further rumination.

B. Morality

The Canon is often seen presenting the author's own opinions of the need for divorce reform through the way many of Holmes' female clients are treated poorly but legally.

Detective Pikachu offers similar messages in its subtext. Throughout there is a message about the dubious morality of forcing Pokémon to fight (see the scenes at The Roundhouse for the most explicit example) and at 64 minutes we see an environmental concern raised when Pikachu asks "At this point, how can you not believe in climate change?"

C. Adventure

In his list, Knox fails to identify the sense of adventure present in the Holmes Canon. The boat chase in The Sign of the Four, the capture of John Clay in The Red-Headed League or the serpentine vigil in The Speckled Band, for example. It is difficult to name a

Canonical story without moments of adventure.

Similarly, Detective Pikachu has many such moments. Major ones would include the flight from the PCL Facility at 60 minutes or the big fight at 84 minutes.

D. Combat

As early as A Study in Scarlet Holmes is identified as "an expert singlestick player, boxer, and swordsman". In The Empty House, we learn he has "some knowledge, however, of baritsu, or the Japanese system of wrestling". And there is no shortage of moments he puts these skills to use. He engages in street brawls in The Final Problem and The Illustrious Client, he sees off Woodley in The Solitary Cyclist and he reveals how he baritsued Moriarty to death in The Empty House.

It is no surprise to see that Pikachu is an equally skilled fighter. He is a master of his electric-type fighting skills as demonstrated in an impressive battle from 80 minutes to 87 minutes.

Far from just being a "pikachu in a hat", this film meets all the Holmesian criteria demanded by Knox and a further four of my own. In conclusion, I restate that Detective Pikachu is the most Canonical movie currently available and is a boon to any Holmesian's DVD collection.

Speedy's by Thinkanddoodle

The Fairy Garden
By Merinda Brayfield

Holmes and I had been acquainted for several years. Despite living with a man so astute in his observations, there were a few things he had missed about me. Part of that was my own obfuscations, but I must admit to a certain pride in evading his gaze.

However, we had reached a crossroads in our cohabitation. Lingering glances had turned into something more. On occasion, he found his way into my bed to sleep. And though I was anxious about his reaction, it was something that must be discussed if we were to proceed.

Holmes slipped in my room near midnight. I was awake, waiting for him. "You've been anxious all evening," he said gently, slipping into bed.

"I have something on my mind," I confessed. "Something I must speak to you about."

He tensed, and I drew him into a kiss. "Not that," I assured him. "I'm quite glad you're here and for what we have."

"Then what is it?" he asked, confusion on his face.

I sat up and put an arm around him. "There in the windowsill, what do you see?" I asked.

He frowned. "Your fairy garden?"

"Keep looking," I said, making a gesture with my hand.

Almost immediately tiny lights appeared, moving among the toadstools and flowers. One of them, a soft purple light, took off and flitted towards us.

"Put out your hand," I told him.

With pure wonder on his face, Holmes obeyed. The tiny creature landed on his palm. "I must be dreaming," he muttered.

"I assure you, you're not," I said softly. I rest my chin on his shoulder. "There are more things in heaven and earth, Holmes, than are dreamt of in your philosophy."

"I... don't understand," he said.

"You do, you just, in this case, don't trust your senses." I reached over to the end table and picked up a bit of biscuit, offering it to the creature. It took the gift and flitted back over to the garden. I made another gesture and the room was once again dark.

"How?" he asked, wonder still heavy in his voice.

"My family has been in these lands a very long time," I said. "There is a gift and a knowledge passed down from generation to generation. I'm by no means the most powerful in my family, but I have enough. This… between us… it would be unfair to continue to hide myself from you. I want to give myself wholeheartedly, and that includes my greatest secret. Traditionally it's only revealed to a suitor just before the wedding."

Holmes blinked a few times. "And if the suitor rejects what they see?"

"Ah," I said, hesitating. "Well…. Magic is useful for a number of things. In the old days murder wasn't unheard of. In these more civilized times, we usually make sure that the person simply forgets."

Holmes turned to look at me, curiosity plain on his face. "I don't wish to forget. Can you teach me?"

I shook my head, taking his elegant hand in my own. "The gift doesn't run in your blood. It would be like trying to teach a dog to speak Latin if you'll forgive the comparison."

Holmes laughed. "No offense taken. I always knew you were a wonder, Watson, but this…"

I squeezed his hand. "This is all of me, Holmes, if you would still have me."

He leaned in and kissed me gently. "I would."

What's in a Holmes?
By iamjohnlocked4life

When posed the question "What makes a Holmes a Holmes?" I'm reminded of that old adage about a rose. No, not the one about goodness giving extras, the other one, that by any other name would smell as sweet. What of the Nearlock Fauxlmes? Should not a Holmes by any other name smell as sweet?

We must begin our investigation by asking: what is a Holmes? The simplest answer is a detective, which is a fairly low bar for entry. By this standard, Lestrade is a Holmes, as are most of the characters in the CSI franchises. And what about Holmeses with other professions? Is Gregory House, M.D., a Holmes? Certainly his character was crafted as a Holmes analogue, down to his punny last name and his companion Wilson. He's engaged in the art of detection, but he investigates symptoms and disease, rather than crime. Perhaps we need to broaden our scope, and consider personality traits rather than professions.

What are the defining characteristics of a Holmes? An analytic mind. Someone who works on the fringes, outside of the conventional structure of their profession. A loner by nature, but one who has found a trusted companion to aid with investigations. A Holmes is a master observer, someone who can see the clues no one else notices, and extrapolate the data to find the answers. A puzzle solver with a thirst for knowledge. In my humble opinion, these are the foundations of the character, though their inverse are sometimes used for comedic effect.

So if it looks like a Holmes and quacks like a Holmes…

But it need not even do that! For what does a Holmes look like? Must a Holmes be a cis white British man? Not if Sara Shelly Futaba (aka Miss Sherlock) has anything to say about it! Or Sara Holmes in the Janet Watson Chronicles. Or Seol-ok in Queen of Mystery. There's a whole slew of diverse female Holmeses that are carrying on the Holmes legacy while innovating with their unique spins on the genre.

A Holmes doesn't even have to be human, as we saw most notably with Basil of Baker Street in The Great Mouse Detective. This wee rodent embodies the spirit of Holmes with his quick wit, dogged tenacity, and a penchant for going undercover with his trusted Dr. Dawson. More recent cartoon adaptations include Sherlock Gnomes, Detective Pikachu, and Sheerluck Holmes in Veggie Tales, as portrayed by an anthropomorphic cucumber [insert Cucumberbatch joke here]. A Holmes can even be a 65 million-year-old reptilian warrior, in the case of Madame Vastra from Doctor Who. Alongside her human wife Jenny, she solves crimes—and occasionally feasts upon criminals—in Victorian London, serving as the inspiration for the Holmes stories in the Whoniverse.

In short, a Holmes can be anything a creator chooses. There need only be intent to craft a protagonist with an inquisitive mind, whose talents and temperament exceed the realm of the average or expected, yet is able to find companionship with a kindred spirit. This archetype is so compelling, its appeal so lasting, that Sherlock Holmes holds the singular honour as the most portrayed literary character in stage, film, and television history. And so I say, let us go forth and create, and spread far and wide the inclusive ethos of No Holmes Barred. All are welcome in our tent, because the bigger the tent, the more Holmeses we have to play with and explore. Embrace the wild, the weird, the silly and the profane, because a Holmes by any name is just as sweet (or snarky, as the case may be).

And perhaps there's something for us here from that other rose quote as well, for to paraphrase Holmes himself, "What a lovely thing a Holmes is!"

Holmes and Asexuality
By Mary-Catherine Berger

Sherlock Holmes has seen many different interpretations in the 133 years since his premier in A Study In Scarlet. He has been female, he has been animated, he has been modernized, etc.; and that's just in officially published works such as BBC's Sherlock or the Sherlock Holmes films with Robert Downey Jr. When delving into the realm of fanfiction, Sherlock Holmes has been interpreted in more ways than is possible to count, in relation to his gender, his country of origin, his backstory, his age, his sexuality, and in countless other ways. Sherlock Holmes has been interpreted as identifying in just about every sexuality that exists, one specifically that should be mentioned is asexuality.

Asexuality is defined as not experiencing sexual attraction, and in many Sherlock Holmes Canon stories, there is evidence to support this interpretation of the beloved character. While we have never seen this represented in a Sherlock adaptation, there is a plethora of fanfictions that are marked as having an asexual Sherlock. However, Sherlock fanfiction with an asexual character often does not give an accurate representation of this complex sexuality. In fanfiction with a tagged asexual Sherlock, we often see a Sherlock who has no interest in sex whatsoever, and it is a conscious choice on his part to abstain from sex.

This is not entirely accurate. Asexuality, as with any sexuality, is not a conscious choice, it is simply how people feel. So these representations do not present asexuality in a truthful light. Even stories that do not show a character in that light will sometimes show them as being entirely sex-repulsed, meaning they find sex disgusting or repulsive. This also does not show asexuality in a truthful way. Asexual people, more commonly referred to as aces, often feel other forms of attraction, these being sensual, aesthetic, and romantic attraction. For example, those who experience demisexuality, a form of asexuality, feel sexual attraction only after building a strong romantic relationship. Those who are autochorissexual, another form of asexuality, don't feel sexual attraction, but are capable of being aroused and are aroused by pornographic content, but not normally in relation to themselves.

Asexuality has many facets and forms, which oftentimes are not displayed in fics that are tagged with asexual characters. Some aces even enjoy sex and have it often, but don't experience sexual attraction, which is a key factor in what makes an asexual an asexual.

This does not necessarily mean that all asexual Sherlock fanfictions are not accurate representations of asexuality, or that they aren't valid interpretations, because for many people, these are representations that they can identify with, which is important in an era that has very little asexual representation. Any asexual representation is good and commendable, but I'd like to highlight how asexual Sherlock fanfictions tend towards a very single minded representation, with very little variety in the forms of asexuality represented. For some, this is due simply to the way that asexuality is represented in popular media, and so it is the way the author believes asexuality is experienced. This is most common in authors who are not asexual themselves. For others, this is simply due to the way that certain people experience asexuality in their own life. And that is acceptable and encouraged, I applaud the authors who are able to bring their own sexuality into their writings.

Asexuality is a complex and often misunderstood sexuality. It can be frustrating for readers who are asexual to read asexual characters that they feel misrepresent them. For those authors who are not asexual, do not be discouraged! Feel free to write your asexual characters, but perhaps consider finding a beta who is asexual. That way you can understand your story from their viewpoint, in addition to your own. For those authors that are asexual, again, I commend you for writing your characters to represent yourselves. And for readers everywhere, of any sexuality, remember that not all asexuals are the same, and asexuality is a vast spectrum of experience and emotion. Don't think there's just one type or one way to be ace, because there are many.

Who Winds the Watches
By #PoetOnaBike

Sunset

A dude on the train
Without ticket or name
Found dead thru the heart
A bullet to blame

Gone 6

A guard was upset
And was all of a sweat
A parasol and six watches.
A body propped and set

3 to 1

Two carriages the scene
One smoking, one clean
Three in and one dead
Makes a mystery too keen

Darkness

A lady and two men
Disappeared where and when
They left him for dead
Will they do it again?

First Light

So on nearby ground
A clue it was downed
All tattered and torn
An old Bible was found

Inscribed

And written within
Names, dates and kin?
John to Alice, then James
Edward, now has-been

2.21

The Detective was called
The papers appalled
Few clues to B found
The case it was stalled

8 to the hour

Sherlock's theory to test
Another train was his quest
With both going slow
A keen jumper the best

Clock stopped

So then found the train
Stationed, it did remain
The express going fifty
Sherlock's efforts in vain

Five years

A stateside letter was sent
But was it worth a cent ?
Said it was James
Saying a Lady was Gent

Rewind

Edward and Sparrow MacCoy
Card-sharping their employ
Dressed to impress
A Lady from a Boy

EST

Mother Alice was so upset
Elder son James a fret
Selling watches a trade
For Edward to forget

GMT

So to England he went
With watches on percent
Sparrow not far behind
And James on their scent

Time to fly

In London, we find
Card tricks are mined
The 'pards flee a scam
Dress-codes reassigned

5 sharp

In that carriage of dread
Awful words are said
A scuffle over a bustle
And a Brother is dead

True time

James says it was his Brother
But this is just a cover
As Sparrow wrote the letter
Brothers lookalike one another

Sunset again

Now the dead dude is James
Sparrow and Edward share shames
They run far far away
And now have new names

New Dawn

Old lives must be burnt
A harsh lesson is learnt
Ideas go around
Honest trade to be earnt

New cycle

Jones and Smith, now they're known
A cycle shop now has grown
Parasols are missed
Whilst tyres must be blown

Doctor Watson and the Unwelcome Critique
A very short and silly radio play
By Vince Stadon

INT. 221b BAKER STREET –
DAY

SFX: knock on door.

WATSON: *(calls out)* Come in, Mrs. Hudson!

GREENHOUGH SMITH: *(muffled)* Dr. Watson?

WATSON: *(calls out)* I am in here, Mrs. Hudson! Do come in, please and—wait! Would you mind saying my name again, please?

GREENHOUGH SMITH: *(muffled)* Not at all. *(clears throat)* Dr. Watson?

WATSON: *(calls out)* Ah! Yes, as I suspected! You are *not* Mrs. Hudson! What have you done with her, you fiend? The good woman was about to bring me breakfast, and I am starving!

GREENHOUGH SMITH: *(muffled)* Err... Your landlady asked me to deliver a message to you, if I might be permitted to come in?

WATSON: *(calls out)* A message? How peculiar. I don't suppose the message comes with a full tray of hot breakfast?

GREENHOUGH SMITH: *(muffled)* No. Look, might I...?

WATSON: *(calls out)* Yes, you had better come in. But I warn you, I am armed!

SFX: door opens, footsteps.

WATSON: Mr. Greenhough Smith! What brings you here from the offices of *The Strand Magazine*?

GREENHOUGH SMITH: Good morning, Dr. Watson. Thank you for permitting me to come in to see you. Finally. I confess to a mild annoyance at being left outside your door for such a tedious exchange of greetings. I was beginning to wonder if it was entirely commonplace for a visitor – an illustrious client, perhaps, or Scotland Yard detective, perchance – to transact their sensitive business in such an eccentric fashion. Furthermore, I would ask you please to immediately desist from *pointing a gun at me!*

WATSON: Yes of course, do excuse me. It is wise to always be on one's guard in my line of business; one never knows what horrors one might be faced with next. Ravenous spectral hounds that rip men to pieces. Deadly snakes. Murderous pygmies. Exploding clowns. Professor Moriarty. The other Professor Moriartys. Scorpions. Assassins. Ex-wives... But of course, as my literary editor, you are well aware of all this.

GREENHOUGH SMITH: Quite. And it is in my capacity as editor for *The Strand* that brings me to your rooms today...

WATSON: Oh? *(delighted)* You have acquiesced to my quite reasonable request for a 200% increase in fees! At last! After all these years! Oh that is most welcome news! This calls for a drink!

GREENHOUGH SMITH: No, I am afraid I am not here to inform you of a raise in your fees; quite the opposite.

WATSON: Oh. No raise? That is most disappointing. I need a drink. Care to join me?

SFX: Watson pours a large drink. Drinks it, pours another.

GREENHOUGH SMITH: It is only eight fifteen in the morning; isn't it a trifle early to be drinking spirits?

WATSON: Not for me. I have a robust constitution. *(belches)*. I think I'll have another. Are you sure you won't have one?

SFX: Watson pours a large drink. Drinks it, pours another.

GREENHOUGH SMITH: Quite sure, thank you. Now before I address the matter which brings me here, perhaps I had better quickly pass on the message I received from your landlady?

WATSON: Of course, Mr. Greenhough Smith, of course. Feel free to pass it on to whomever you please.

GREENHOUGH SMITH: The message--

WATSON: *(interrupting)* In however a manner you wish to convey it. You might print the message in *The Strand Magazine*, or send a telegram, or enlist carrier pigeons, or--

GREENHOUGH SMITH: *(interrupting)* The message is for *you*, Doctor Watson, and since I am here in this room with you, and since I have quite ably demonstrated my abilities to verbally communicate with you, I think it would be simpler if I just *tell* you the message, and it is this: "You owe three months' rent. Until it is paid in full, there will be no breakfast, or any other meal, beverage, or urgent telegram from Scotland Yard, delivered to your rooms."

WATSON: *(anguished)* Three months' rent? No meals delivered? I need a drink!

SFX: Watson pours a large drink. Drinks it, pours another.

GREENHOUGH SMITH: And now that we have dispensed with that trifle, I--

WATSON: *(interrupting)* Please do not mention trifles, Mr. Greenhough Smith, or indeed, any other food. My stomach could not bear the disappointment.

GREENHOUGH SMITH: I shall do my best to avoid mentioning food, Dr. Watson. I stake my reputation on it.

WATSON: *(groans)* Steak!

GREENHOUGH SMITH: Forgive me. Let us move swiftly on to more fruitful matters.

WATSON: *(groans)* Fruit!

GREENHOUGH SMITH: Doctor Watson, *The Strand Magazine* has been publishing your Sherlock Holmes stories for many years now, and-- look, would you mind closing the windows? I'm finding it difficult to concentrate as it's rather chilly in here.

WATSON: *(groans)* Chilli!

SFX: window is closed.

GREENHOUGH SMITH: Thank you. As I was saying, we have adopted a new, and much more rigorous editorial policy at *Strand Magazine*, and I'm afraid to say I'm going to have to ask you to be much more careful, much more precise with the details and facts of your stories. *(beat)* I take it that you have no objection to this?

WATSON: I'm sorry, I wasn't listening. When I closed the window, I caught a glimpse of the Langham Hotel across the street, and my mind wandered. I was imagining myself sat at a table at the Langham's first-rate dining room, about to tuck in to a sumptuous three-course meal.

GREENHOUGH SMITH: Has the Langham Hotel moved overnight?

WATSON: No, of course not. *(mocking)* You can't just move one of London's most prestigious hotels in the course of an evening: that would be impossible! Have you lost your mind, Mr. Greenhough Smith? Drinking too much, perhaps?

GREENHOUGH SMITH: I was about to enquire such a thing of you, doctor. For the Langham Hotel is not now, and never has been, situated opposite this house.

WATSON: It isn't?

GREENHOUGH SMITH: No.

WATSON: Well, where is it then?

GREENHOUGH SMITH: The Langham Hotel, as its name suggests, is on Langham Street.

WATSON: Yes, now you come to mention it... you're absolutely right. I don't know what I was thinking. The lack of food perhaps caused a temporary lapse in concentration. I'll have a drink: that will help sharpen my senses.

SFX: Watson pours a large drink. Drinks it, pours another.

GREENHOUGH SMITH: It is precisely this sort of inattention to fact that is the root of the problem with your Sherlock Holmes stories, and which I insist must be immediately addressed if *Strand Magazine* is to continue publishing them.

WATSON: What are you saying? Are you suggesting that there are factual errors in the stories I submit to you?

GREENHOUGH SMITH: That is precisely what I am saying.

WATSON: Then you are talking nonsense, Mr. Greenhough Smith; complete and utter tripe. *(beat)*. Tripe! *(beat)* You see, sir, I was actually there, with Mr. Sherlock Holmes, offering my invaluable assistance and expert opinions, throughout all the cases I have submitted for publication. Whereas you sir, were not there. *(beat, momentarily unsure)* You weren't there, were you? *(certain now)* No, you were not there. Nobody from *Strand Magazine* was there. Only *I* was there. Me, sir. Dr. Watson. I am therefore uniquely placed to record for posterity the details of these cases, and... and further... furthermore only *I* can know with absolute certainty what quantifies as a fact, and what does not! *(hiccups)* Excuse me. So what do you have to say to that?

GREENHOUGH SMITH: I do not doubt that you were assisting Mr. Sherlock Holmes in his cases. I merely cast suspicion on the accuracy of your reportage of them.

WATSON: This is ridiculous, and I need a drink.

SFX: Watson pours a large drink. Drinks it, pours another.

GREENHOUGH SMITH: Let us take, as an example, the case you submitted to us under the title of the *Adventure of the Second Stain.*

WATSON: What about it?

GREENHOUGH SMITH: You persist that it is a truly factual account of what happened?

WATSON: Every word, every comma.

GREENHOUGH SMITH: *The Second Stain* is set entirely in London, is it not, and the case pertains to sensitive governmental matters?

WATSON: Absolutely.

GREENHOUGH SMITH: Well then perhaps you could tell me why it details towns and streets that don't exist anywhere in England, and politicians who have never held office in this country.

WATSON: Err... Um. Hang about... let me think. Er... I'd better have a drink, it helps my, er, memory.

GREENHOUGH SMITH: And then there is the Jefferson Hope murder case, when you first met Sherlock Holmes. Do you recall it?

SFX: Watson pours a large drink. Drinks it, pours another.

WATSON: I recall it with perfect clarity like it was this morning.

GREENHOUGH SMITH: It *is* the morning. You titled this one, *A Study in Scarlet*.

WATSON: Good title that. Catchy. Was thinking about a sequel. *A Study in Aubergine.*

GREENHOUGH SMITH: In *A Study in Scarlet*, the villain of the piece, Mr. Jefferson Hope, refuses to come to 221b Baker Street because he suspects, quite rightly, that a trap has been laid for him by the cunning Sherlock Holmes.

WATSON: That's right, yes. Suspicious fellow he was, Jefferson Hope.

GREENHOUGH SMITH: Was he also suffering from amnesia?

WATSON: No of course not.

GREENHOUGH SMITH: Well then how do you explain the fact that twenty-four hours later he seemingly forgets all his suspicions, and turns up at 221b Baker Street?

WATSON: Um...

GREENHOUGH SMITH: Moreover, Jefferson Hope, half-dead by an aneurysm, recovers instantly and needs to be restrained by four men. I can only assume that in addition to his amnesia, he suddenly developed inexplicable superhuman abilities.

WATSON: Er...

GREENHOUGH SMITH: Perhaps you yourself are possessed of remarkable physiological qualities?

WATSON: *(chuckles)* Well, there are one or two young ladies who might well say so! *(clears throat)* But why do you ask?

GREENHOUGH SMITH: I ask if your body is unique because I can think of no other explanation as to why the Jezail bullet with which you were wounded from the campaign in Afghanistan seems to move from your shoulder, as you report in one story, to your leg, as you report it in another, and then your Achilles tendon, as reported in a third story.

WATSON: Ah. I see. Well, um... err... I can explain that one. Let me muse on the matter as I have a drink.

SFX: Watson pours a large drink. Drinks it, pours another.

GREENHOUGH SMITH: Perhaps while you muse on that matter you might also give consideration to a few others. Such as the rather bizarre way June jumps into September within a few hours in *The Sign of the Four*.

WATSON: Does it? Gosh.. um... that's um... err...

GREENHOUGH SMITH: Or the fact that your wife doesn't seem to know your name, and insists on calling you James.

WATSON: What? Which wife?

GREENHOUGH SMITH: *(sighs)* Dr. Watson, your Sherlock Holmes stories are riddled with errors of continuity, blunders of narrative, and sloppy, not to say downright dishonest reportage of the facts, and yet... and yet you still maintain that you are recording them faithfully, based on your notes? Tell me, Dr. Watson, do you often drink when you are writing?

WATSON: Yes of course - helps get the creative juices flowing, and all that.

GREENHOUGH SMITH: Well then, that would explain everything.

WATSON: *(irked)* I'm not sure it does. And I'm not sure I care for your tone. In fact -- yes, fact! -- in fact I am not sure I care for you one bit, Mr. Greengrocer Smith!

GREENHOUGH SMITH: Greenhough Smith.

WATSON: *(enraged)* You burst into our rooms without so much as a by your leave, threatening me with no breakfast, refusing to give me a raise, ordering me to disarm myself, and raiding my Tantalus! You accuse me of dishonesty, sloppiness, moving an hotel from one location to another, and having a remarkable body, none of which is remotely true. *(beat)* No, hang on, the last bit is true -- the body thing, but the rest of it is complete and utter twaddle of the highest order. Now I have a blinding headache, a rumbling stomach, and an urge to reach for my revolver and march you out the door at gunpoint!

GREENHOUGH SMITH: Oh dear! I am afraid I have enraged you.

WATSON: You have done more than enrage me, Mr. Greenfingerson--

GREENHOUGH SMITH: Greenhough Smith.

WATSON: You have made me extremely angry!

GREENHOUGH SMITH: Err, isn't that what enraged means?

WATSON: Well you should know sir, seeing as you are an editor!

GREENHOUGH SMITH: I do know. And it does.

WATSON: Well then!

GREENHOUGH SMITH: I think this little jape has gone too far. I can only apologise, Dr. Watson.

WATSON: Jape? What do you mean? And I did ask you to stop mentioning food.

GREENHOUGH SMITH: I wasn't aware that was such a foodstuff as jape.

WATSON: No, you're right. I meant grape. I got confused for a moment. When I was, err, enraged.

GREENHOUGH SMITH: When you were extremely angry, you mean?

WATSON: Yes. Then. But I have composed myself, and I shall feel much better after a drink and an explanation. You say this is all some kind of jape?

SFX: Watson pours a large drink. Drinks it, pours another.

GREENHOUGH SMITH: Yes, I'm afraid so. A practical joke. I was asked to come here this morning and play a little jape on you. I do apologise, it was never my intention to, err, enrage you.

WATSON: Who asked you to do this? What kind of cruel and heartless fiend would put you up to this and deny a man a peaceful breakfast?

GREENHOUGH SMITH: Mr. Sherlock Holmes.

WATSON: Holmes?

GREENHOUGH SMITH: He paid me handsomely and assured me you would take the thing in good spirits. In fact he said you would almost certainly be likely to *literally* take the thing in good spirits, and wagered that you would help yourself to six full glasses of scotch.

WATSON: Did he indeed? The swine! Well he is wrong, for I have had *ten* full glasses of scotch!

GREENHOUGH SMITH: He said you would say that, and has asked me to inform you that he has been watering down the scotch, meaning that ten full glasses is really only six.

WATSON: Damn him! But wait - the message from Mrs. Hudson... was that part of the ruse?

GREENHOUGH SMITH: No, that was genuine.

WATSON: *(mournfully)* This is terrible! I owe three months' rent, and worse, have to forego breakfast!

GREENHOUGH SMITH: However, I am pleased to be able to tell you that Strand Magazine has gladly agreed to increase your fee, by 200%

WATSON: Really? You really mean it? For real? *(hiccups)*

GREENHOUGH SMITH: On the condition that you avail yourself of a thesaurus. *(beat)* That, err, was a joke.

WATSON: 200%?

GREENHOUGH SMITH: Backdated. I have the cheque with me.

WATSON: This is... I don't know what to say... I don't know how to thank you...

GREENHOUGH SMITH: Well, you could offer to buy me breakfast?

WATSON: A splendid idea! Breakfast at the Langham! But first... let's have a drink.

<u>END</u>

Letters to Santa We Would Like to See
by Wanda and Jeff Dow

Dear Santa,

Just a clue. Maybe a couple, but at least one.

Your Friend,
Inspector Lestrade

> Dear St. Nick,
>
> I ask this for my new husband, not myself. He has lost his job and his strength all in the same month. A few bottles of Serum of Anthropoid would be of great help.
>
> Sincerely,
> Alice Morphy Presbury

Dear Santa,

What I would really like is a very quiet remainder of the academic year.

Respectfully,
Dr. Thorneycroft Huxtable.

Dear Santa Claus,

I really need a very good book of insults-preferably of obscure ones or ones that no one will understand.

Yours,
Dr. Grimesby Roylott

Dear St. Nick,

I know I am a little old to believe in you, but I could really use someone to talk to.

Affectionately,
Laura Lyons

Dear Santa,

I know I speak for all the directors when I sincerely request that you supply us with a list of excellent concrete contractors. Expense is no limit.

Eagerly awaiting your reply,
Lucius Merryweather

No Holmes Barred
By Robert Perret

Tunalock
By Samuel Verner

"Once upon a time someone created an alternative universe.
This has made a lot of people very angry and has been widely regarded as a bad move."
- Douglas Adams, sort of.

Alternative Universes are described as a fanwork which changes one or more elements of the source work's canon. Technically, this includes anything that isn't faithful to the original canon itself, such as movies, films, basically anything that deviates from the original storyline in any way. In this light, there are quite a few works with Alternative Universes written and popularized about them, such as Greek mythologies, folklore, and many famous stories, all of which have had countless adaptations and stories written about them, which contain barely a sliver from the original source. The Hunchback of Notre Dame, Three Musketeers, and several Disney movies spring to mind.

Well-loved tales are frequently changed, and the stories retold in new ways as they explore the essential aspects of the characters, preserving their essence while still creating something entirely new. The Adventures of Sherlock Holmes, well known around the world, are no exception. Holmes has been reincarnated as a mouse (The Great Mouse Detective), a hound (Sherlock Hound), and has even fought dinosaurs (Asylum's Sherlock Holmes). Jumping from the past to the future, Dr. John Watson has been a cyborg (Sherlock Holmes in the 20th Century), and they have both been set against fantastical creatures like vampires and zombies (Victorian Undead by Ian Edginton). The characters have been written to exist in different parts of the world, in different universes and time periods, and made to interact with famous characters from other tales. Stories, both published and unpublished, have explored countless themes and storylines, with more being written every day.

Unpublished fiction (fanfiction) has been a realm where writers, both new and old, can play with different styles and themes, mixing and matching them with the joy of creating a collage of artwork in literary form. While some AUs have been published and well-known, these are just the tip of the iceberg of the rich field of imagination and character exploration unpublished fiction has explored.

"Percy Jackson," "Harry Potter," Disney and Marvel have explored stories with mythological beings, and Sherlock writers, never ones to shy away from any topic, have transformed Sherlockian characters into angels, demons, shapeshifters, and fauns. Fauns (or satyrs) are half-goat, half-human beings from Ancient Roman mythology. They have been portrayed in tales as being spiritual guides to gods of the forest. In the Percy Jackson series, a faun was a guide for the main character in the story. One of the most well-known fairies from old English mythology, Puck, who featured in one of Shakespeare's plays, "A Midsummer Night's Dream," has also been historically portrayed as a faun. So, what better mythological fodder for retelling and alternate universe exploration with Sherlock Holmes then that of old English mythology?

With each generation, each person brings their favorite Holmes, should this be as out there as The Great Mouse Detective or as wide-reaching as Dr. Gregory House. More recent adaptations have brought life to the fandom and an outpouring of imaginative exploration of the stories and characters. As such, recent stories often hold aspects and character traits that are influenced by favored adaptations. Fanfictions of a televised fanfiction, holding qualities from the original Canon stories, the televised series, or a mix of both. Inspiration that spurs the writing muses to encourage the telling of the Sherlockian characters in many settings. Several of the recent stories and faunlock imaginings have reflected more recent televised adaptations.

Unfortunately, while alternative universes are frequently written, and the exploration of different themes and mythologies is common, there are always those who despair if stories reach out beyond a set net, which they personally condone. Attempts to stifle the age-old practice of story retelling and exploration of characters and settings were considered, and Tunalock was hatched. For no response is more fitting to a ridiculous complaint then a more ridiculous answer.

Tunalock, in all its glory, is exactly what it sounds like. Sherlock Holmes as a tuna. Sometimes with legs, but often not, it is one of the most openly and freely ridiculous AUs that could be conceived, but certainly far from the only one. The hound and the mouse adaptations seem logical when one compares them to how Holmes has also been portrayed in fanfiction as a peacock, a swan, and an F-16 Fighting Falcon.

Initially conceived as a joke amongst friends, and attributed to the lovely imagination of 'villain-in-training,' Tunalock falls within the wonderful realm that is 'crack fic.' Crack fic is a category of fanfiction that purposely delves into the utterly absurd. Defined as 'fanworks with a fundamentally ludicrous premise', these stories are written as comedy, parody, or occasionally merely humor and because one can. Tunalock is an amusing concept that has since been embraced by fans with artwork from many countries. Artists including 'ivorylungs' 'sasananao3', 'ofcowardiceandkings', and 'skylanth' have joined in the fun with various fan-created works.

An excerpt from 'not-the-very-button':

"The greatest thing about Tuna!lock though, is that people have taken the bait, so to speak.
Those individuals who lump the Sherlock fandom under one misrepresentational umbrella automatically assume that there must be people seriously and un-ironically loving this thing. They express their "disgust" at the Sherlockians. They "lose all their respect" for Sherlock fans. Which is a joke in itself, because if they can genuinely believe that Tuna!lock is for real? They obviously never had any respect for the Sherlock fandom to begin with."

Hundreds of adaptations of Sherlock Holmes has been made through the years, with countless changes and deviations from the original Canon made. From film to fanfiction, no aspect of the original stories had not been changed in some way by someone while creating their own Sherlockian fan work, and the practice continues as more tales, adaptations and artwork continues to be made. Sherlockians are a colorful and inventive kettle of fish that take joy in exploring and experimenting with the vast seas of possibilities, all hatched from the shared enjoyment of Canon all that is Sherlockiania. The only limit to any interpretation being one's own imagination.

As long as stories exist, so too will Alternative Universes, offshoot stories and new adaptations and imaginings. Whether someone likes it or not, whether it fits their view of what aspects of stories they like retold or it doesn't (which tends to be quite arbitrary within itself once examined), humans are imaginative and artistic creatures, and one hopes that someday the close-minded few who are trapped in their boxes and set views of what should and shouldn't be, based on their own limited perceptions, may someday be able to expand outside of their shell to embrace the imaginations and interpretations of others outside of themselves.

The grand ocean of fandom would be a very boring place indeed if people were restrained to a tiny fish bowl, locked in with but a few standardized plastic selections for a backdrop.

The Greatest Achievement Ever Made
in a *Holmes & Watson* Film:
Holmes & Watson
By Brad Keefauver

The year was 2018.

The country had fallen into dysthymia over the events of the year just past. It didn't even matter which English-speaking country that referred to, as the mere fact that they could hear what was being said in English during 2018 was enough to infect them with that mild depression.

In February of that year, John Christopher Reilly, actor and practitioner of transcendental meditation, had walked the red carpet at London's Cineworld Empire Leicester Square theatre for his portrayal of Hank Marlow, the last survivor of a World War II aerial squadron, in the movie *Kong: Skull Island*.

In the April that followed, James Joyce award winner, John William Ferrell was riding in a sport utility vehicle that overturned in a serious collision, and was taken to the hospital. He was released unharmed.

It had been one hundred and thirty years since Sir Arthur Conan Doyle created the characters of John H. Watson and Sherlock Holmes for the British reading public. Little could Doyle have foreseen that these two Americans, one a dapper Hollywood actor, the other an auto accident victim, would breathe new and unexpected life into his oft-neglected creations in that far future time.

Had he known, Doyle's well-remembered words to actor William Hooker Gillette, "You may marry him, or murder or do what you like with him," might have been more simply expressed: "Do that, sir! Do that!"

But William Gillette had neither reliable film sound synchronization nor director Etan Cohen to assist him in his attempts to bring Sherlock Holmes to life in the cinema. Gillette's 1916 film attempt, directed by Arthur Berthelet, only had the name "Holmes" in its title and was lost for almost a century, as only the French had the attention span to retain a copy, and did not bother to tell anyone until 2014. Were Gillette to have seen what would be achieved using the character of Sherlock Holmes in that far future release of Christmas 2018, it is safe to say that he might have given up his attempt then and there.

But no time machine traveler could have made a man of that day fully understand the nuance and deep interpretation that movie-makers of the 2010s could apply to adapting the great detective. In fact, even screenwriter and eventual director Etan Cohen could not have foreseen the results when he first began putting words to paper in 2008. The character of Sherlock Holmes had been in true doldrums since 1994, when actor Jeremy Brett had finished parroting the Conan Doyle texts. Popular superhero actors Robert Downey Jr. and Benedict Cumberbatch had yet to take their turns as Holmes, and the theatrical horizon seemed gray indeed for Mr. Sherlock Holmes. Could a Sherlock Holmes comedy revive the world's greatest detective?

Judd Apatow, the visionary comic filmmaker of the new millennium, seemed to think so. His vision, as reported in the Hollywood scandal sheets of 2008, was to take Etan Cohen's script, cast Sacha Baron Cohen (no relation) as Sherlock Holmes, and add a few more millions to the coffers of the Sony media conglomerate via its Columbia Pictures label. John William Ferrell, better known as "Will" Ferrell was touted as Cohen's Watson for the film.

For eight long years, the project dwelt in the purgatory known by industry insiders as "development hell." Sacha Baron Cohen would become involved in writing and producing his own films, *Bruno* and *The Dictator*. It was reported by a prominent London newspaper that Judd Apatow once vowed to include a penis in every motion picture he filmed. Whether the result of those events or others, both men fell away from the project, but Etan Coen and Will Ferrell stayed on.

In November of 2016 various key cast members were hired, and a month later filming on the movie began at Shepperton Studios in Surrey, England. (Those same studios that had served in the filming of *2001: A Space Odyssey, Star Wars, Blade Runner,* and, one day, *Detective Pikachu.*)

On November 14, 2016, Screen Actors Guild award winner Dorothea Lauren Allegra Lapkus was cast to play the woman who would inspire Sherlock Holmes beyond all previous women in his life, Millie. An Inspector Lestrade was found in Robert Brydon Jones, MBE. Kelly Macdonald, an Emmy award winner with a theater named after her, became Mrs. Hudson. And need I even go into the acclaim of actors Rebecca Hall, Ralph Fiennes, or Hugh Laurie? I think not.

Film crews were seen at Hampton Court Palace, one of King Henry the Eighth's two surviving palaces, a gift to him from a disgraced cardinal in 1529. The symbol of such a grand royal gift used in the filming of a movie surely inspired the crew with a feeling that they, too, were creating a grand gift to the world. And they did.

Alan Menken, one of the handful of people ever to win Academy Awards, Grammy Awards, a Tony Award, and an Emmy Award, wrote what has been called a "full-throated love song" for Sherlock Holmes and John H. Watson. It's lyricist, Glenn Slater, described it as follows: "It begins in a musical theater, almost Rex Harrison kind of way, and then turns into a full-on, '70s pop/soft rock love extravaganza, with an operatic interlude in the middle." The song would come to be hailed by many as the greatest part of the film that would showcase it.

Multi-instrumentalist Mark Allen Mothersbaugh was enlisted to do the full soundtrack for the film being constructed, having risen from band leader with a cult following to successful soundtrack artist, beloved for such works as the score to *Thor: Ragnarok*, destined to ring in the Valhalla of Nordic symphonic work for a very long time.

The finished film, given the title *Holmes & Watson*, was set to be released on August 3 of 2018. Seemingly intimidated by what could happen when they did bestow this incredible gift upon an unwary public, Sony Pictures delayed the release to November 9, 2018, but let a trailer come out on September 28 to forewarn those alert to such things. It became apparent from that day forward that the sort of misunderstood genius only grasped be a select few had been achieved, and Sony delayed the film's release yet again to December 21, 2018, and then, one more time, realizing that Christmas Day itself was the only day that such gifts to humanity could be given.

Was this film, *Holmes & Watson*, the cinematic equivalent of that sweet Baby Jesus, also given to the world on that day? Would both wise men and shepherds come to theaters, drawn by a star named Will Ferrell to offer their gifts of ticket monies and concession purchases? And would the film then be judged by unworthies in the tradition of Pontius Pilate, flogged, condemned to death, and then crucified by an uncaring world?

The parallels might give one cause to think.

This cinematic child of a gracious Hollywood won at least four golden awards, despite the cruel injustices imposed upon it, and it inspired its followers to look more kindly upon all movies of Sherlock Holmes and John H. Watson. Some even gathered under the name "Doyle's Rotary Coffin" to spread their new creed of "No Holmes Barred!"

If the year 2018 is remembered for nothing else in the *Historie Sherlockian*, it will be remembered for that unbelievable film, *Holmes and Watson*, the likes of which we had never seen before, and would not likely see ever again.

The Adventure of the March Hare
By Amy Thomas

"Would you stop with that endless clicking?"

I lifted my fingers from my steno machine, eyebrow raised. "You're the writer, Johnny. I'd have thought you'd appreciate an accurate record of our conversations."

My friend, still clad in his thrifted suit even though billable hours were long over, bristled slightly. "Depositions. Hearings. Arbitrations. That's what I need you for. Not to sit there typing like Nellie Bly while we're having a friendly discussion."

I slowly put my machine aside. "As you wish, but I do hope you're aware that the celebrated Elizabeth Cochran Seaman, pen name Nellie Bly, was a journalist, not a court reporter." I spoke as one does when one wishes to particularly savor one's point.

Johnny rubbed his eyes with exaggerated slowness. "Quite frankly, I wish she was here now, because you're not helping."

"Testy, testy," I muttered. "You're stealing my role as irritant in this partnership."

This statement elicited a tight-lipped smile from my housemate. "I need help," he said. "Real help. The State won't offer a deal, and I don't want this in front of a jury. Bail was practically miraculous."

"Are you sure he's actually innocent?" I asked.

"You can interview him yourself."

"That won't do if we're to maintain my role as a disinterested court reporter," I answered, "but I'd like to be there while you do it."

So it was that the next day I turned up to Johnny's law office, clad in my usual gray hound's-tooth skirt and black blazer, pulling my steno machine in a rolling bag behind me. "Good morning," I said to the paralegal, Mrs. Harmon, who, as usual, pulled a granola bar from the environs of her desk before ushering me into the conference room.

"You look thinner than ever," she said. "I swear you court reporters never eat." She pressed the blueberry chocolate monstrosity into my hands.

"It's a talent one acquires after years of being denied lunch breaks by attorneys," I said drily. Not that it had ever bothered me a great deal not to eat.

I took my place at the head of the long wooden table in the conference room and set up my machine, my pumps raking across the texture of the gray carpet.

My phone vibrated, and I unlocked it. *Witness interview tomorrow. Can you cover?*

Witness statements are not usually recorded by court reporters. At best, audio recordings are made, and overworked transcriptionists with no legal experience at all spit out a record replete with errors for a far cheaper price than anything a self-respecting reporter would generate.

I can I texted back tersely. Jeff Lester could be as annoying as heck, but he was thorough, and he knew who to ask for help when he was beside himself, which happened so often he might as well have cell divided into two people. Recording his interviews wasn't about a record; it was about having a reason for me to be in the room.

"Sharon," Johnny nodded to me as he walked into the conference room with his bail-bonded client, back to his usual good humor after his frustration of the previous day. The client was a middle-aged man with brown hair and thin fingers. I looked at him quickly, taking care to smile while I did so for the sake of social acceptability.

"This is the court reporter," John explained. "She's going to take down everything we say here today. It will help you get ready for your deposition that's coming up."

"Okay," said the man, very softly.

I noted that he did not appear to find this odd, an indication that he had little experience with the legal process. A frequent flyer would have known that deposition preparation is the last place one would normally find a court reporter. We're too expensive to be wasted on practice sessions.

John took out the list of questions I'd written for him. I hadn't done it because I thought he was an incompetent lawyer. He wasn't the most remarkable, but he was thorough and knew his profession. However, he'd already had his chance with the client and gotten his questions answered. My list contained the things I wanted to see the man answer for myself. Watching the way things were said would be, for me, at least as important as the words, if not far more.

After a few preliminary questions about the man's background and education, the real show commenced. "All right, Mr. Lewis, you're here because the police allegedly found you on May 14th, covered in blood and standing over the body of Laura Anderson. Is that what happened?"

"Yes."

Johnny nodded. "We won't dispute the reports of Officer Carmichael or the paramedic."

Even breathing. Hands loosely folded. Mouth slack. Lewis was certainly not made nervous or anxious by the recollection of his tragedy. Worth noting, though on its own inconclusive, because repetition over weeks and months of interviews could desensitize anyone to anything.

"You've seen the photos," my friend continued, producing printouts. The usual crime-scene stuff. I'd looked through them as soon as Johnny had taken the case, but now I watched Lewis look through them again. Nothing terribly peculiar there. He appeared exactly as repulsed as a normal person could be expected to be by viewing a stabbing victim, no more nor less.

He hadn't, he claimed, known the victim at all. And he did not show the grief of a loved one.

The thing went on in this way. Lewis had come home to find Anderson dead on his floor, very recently dead, if one synthesized the report of the examiner, and had become bloodied from trying to help. And therein was John's problem. No one else had materialized in any kind of proximity to have done it before Lewis had arrived home. And no one, his neighbors claimed, had heard anything strange at all.

Circumstantial, certainly, but the state attorney knew as well as Johnny did that juries had convicted on inconvenient circumstances plenty of times. No deal had been forthcoming because the State would lose nothing by trial, while Lewis stood to lose everything.

"Well?"

Johnny reached home a couple of hours after I did, and by then I had a rough transcript of the interview printed and my thin Liliput fountain pen at the ready to make notes. "It occurs to me that this is a sort of locked room mystery," I murmured, "a locked property mystery. I need to see Lewis's house."

"Of course, if you want to," said Johnny. "Did you—get anything from today?"

"Lewis is a terrible liar," I said. "Did you notice how he reacted to the question about his past relationships?"

"He said he's never had a relationship last more than three months," said John quizzically. "That checks out with his history."

"His history as he gave it to you," I retorted, circling the related line on my transcript. "Look at his hands. I noticed it on the video you sent me of his first interview when he was panning through the photographs. That's why I threw in the relationship question."

Johnny thought for a moment. "His hands are...calloused?"

"There's an indentation on his ring finger," I said quickly. "He used to wear a ring, for long enough that it left a mark that never fully went away. If he hasn't been married, he's been in a relationship serious enough for some kind of ring-bound commitment."

"Class ring?" Johnny countered.

"Then why stop wearing it?" I asked. "I would be more likely to admit the possibility if he hadn't been so utterly unconvincing when he was lying about it," I added. "Gaze shifting around the room, slight tremor in the voice, heavy breathing—he's lying, and he's worried about you finding out."

"Why didn't the neighbors say anything different, then?" Johnny was reaching for his last resort.

"He'd only lived there for two months before the murder. They barely knew him, and they wouldn't have had reason to necessarily know his romantic history, especially since, as you yourself have said, all of their interview statements agree that it was a neighborhood where everyone kept to themselves."

Johnny sighed and ran his hand over his face. "I should give up on his innocence, then?"

"Certainly not," I replied. "I think he's far more credible now that I've seen how poorly he lies. My abilities don't extend to clairvoyance, so I can't tell you the reason for the specific deception, but I am reasonably convinced he didn't murder Laura Anderson."

My friend sighed again. "You'll be the death of me in the end. I thought you were about to tell me to give up the case."

I looked up from my now-notated transcript. "I do not disparage your skills as a litigator. If the man were guilty of the crime the State has pinned on him, you'd have known it, even if our means of arriving at the same point would have been quite different."

He nodded once. "But still," he added, "I don't like when my clients lie to me, not this blatantly. I'd rather be their priest-like confessor, even if what I have to hear is uncomfortable. Or, at least, I wish I had your skills. They can never lie to you—not really."

Johnny wasn't looking at me and didn't see my wry half smile. What he considered my wondrous gifts had caused me no end of irritation, at the least, and heartache, at the most, since their emergence during my late childhood. Being able to slice through the deceptive follies of others is a much-lauded gift if one wishes to help the law in the apprehension of the guilty and exoneration of the innocent, but it's less welcome the rest of the time. Not that I would trade my abilities for anything.

The next day, I recorded a deadly dull zoning meeting before making my way further downtown to the office of Detective Jeff Lester, on the second floor in the middle of the Major Crimes Division. The department, like most other police departments in middle America, could only afford one administrative assistant, so Lester ushered me in himself, and I found his office just as organized and unimaginative as ever, exemplary of a man whose conventionality made him excel at the procedure and tedium of his job while floundering at anything requiring original thought.

"The witness is a morgue attendant at Midtown General. He called in a couple of days ago to the main information line, said he thought a body had gone missing. The weird ones get routed to me, the ones nobody at the lower level wants to deal with."

I set up my steno on Lester's tiny faux wooden table while he talked, but I wasn't too distracted to note the pride in his voice.

He feigned annoyance, but in reality he loved being the go-to receptacle of the strange and difficult. Especially now that he had a lateral brain—my lateral brain—to consult.

Within a few minutes, the bottom floor buzzed Lester saying the witness had arrived, and he went to show the man in. I arranged myself professionally. There was always a chance a witness might question why, if they had any experience of the legal system, a court reporter was even present, but few ever had.

This witness certainly did not. He was lean and earnest and spun a tale of a missing corpse that sounded like someone writing Edgar Allan Poe fanfiction. He'd received a body in the morgue— stabbing victim, no identification, pronounced dead nearly immediately after reaching the emergency room.

According to hospital policy, he'd logged receipt of the body on the shared database and then gone to his break. At this point, even recounting the story made him turn pale. "There— there wasn't anything there, Sir. Her place was empty, and when I logged into the computer, the record was gone. I—don't understand. I asked my boss. He said nothing had happened. I tried to escalate it upward in the hospital, but everyone said I was crazy. They made me take a drug test. I'm not crazy, Sir. That's why I'm here now."

To his credit, Lester had a good witness-side manner. "No one's doubting your desire to help," he said mildly. "We'll certainly look into this, but we won't do anything to jeopardize your job."

Suggestions of a hospital cover-up. I was certainly intrigued. Lester smiled at me; he knew this sounded like exactly the kind of case I liked very much. The fact that it had occurred on the same night that Charles Lewis had found a dead woman in his vestibule? That was a coincidence that gave me pause.

If only Lewis had lived in an apartment building, I thought that night as I drove to his house. Apartments are noisy and horrible and make it impossible for anyone to do anything entirely in secret. But instead he lived in a house in one of those insidious little suburbs where things happen in secret all the time, and no one ever seems to know anything about anyone else's business, except when there's nothing helpful in the knowing.

I would have appealed to Lester if needed, but Johnny had no trouble getting access for me under the guise of being part of the "legal team," which wasn't entirely untrue. I chose late hours to arrive, the less likely to alarm the neighbors, who were on high alert since a bona fide murder had been perpetrated in their midst. More's the pity they hadn't always been so observant, I thought, though not bitterly. I had long since learned to expect little of the average human's observational abilities.

Johnny had agreed not to come with me, convinced by my sincere argument that whatever he had already seen and deduced would only serve to cloud and distract my own judgment. I parked my Honda a couple of blocks away and walked over to the house, which must have, at the time of the incident, looked like every other single-family domicile on the street, but now had overgrown landscaping and drooping police tape as its dismal ornaments.

I had with me my bag, flashlight, magnifier, and notebook. Nothing fancy desired or needed. My only other armaments were the questions I wanted answered.

I was not a trained detective, nor did I have any official forensic qualifications. My particular brand of consultation had arisen entirely out of native skill and personal inquiry. I formulated questions to answer, and then I pursued the facts until I found the answers I sought. I neither knew nor cared how people like Lester had learned their jobs; I only knew my own methods.

I felt adrenaline coursing through me. Even though the scene had long lay dormant, and I did not expect to uncover any fresh forensic evidence, my proximity to the epicenter of the case made me feel like I was on the scent at last, no stenography machine needed.

I stepped across tape and into the house, recalling the notes I had read about Lewis's account of the evening and the police's. Lewis claimed he had come home at the normal time from his work as a banking manager and stopped for a hamburger on the way. He'd come home, opened the door, and screamed at the sight of Laura Anderson in the doorway.

No one, or so they claimed, had seen or heard anything unusual until that scream. His neighbor had called the police on her cell phone and run over, corroborating the allegation that Lewis had been found with blood all over him. Why had he touched the body? He said he'd wanted to check for a pulse and other vitals, a story that was more or less plausible given that he'd taken first aid training and theoretically had the skills.

Unfortunately for Lewis, the 911 neighbor couldn't swear that she'd seen him pull into his garage, or even that she had any idea whether he'd been home or not for the evening. One neighbor across the street said she thought maybe he hadn't been; another said he had.

The main problem for the State, the fact that Lewis had hardly acted like a cold-blooded killer in any respect, had been quickly overshadowed by how preposterous it appeared that anyone else could have done it. Probability, when it isn't absolute, is not certainty, but it can appear so to many people.

I took brief note of where the body and Lewis had been found in the front vestibule, before walking through the house with flashlight illuminating my steps. I forced myself to reject the expected, to view this house as the only house in the world. It would help me not at all to think of it in terms of all the other similar houses or suburbs.

One floor. Three bedrooms. Two bathrooms. Front door. Back door. Garage. Supposedly, nothing in the house had been moved. Lewis had made bail, but he'd moved in with a friend for the sake of the ongoing investigation, and the police had only taken what they thought they needed for testing, leaving the rest as it was.

Of course, there had been countless uniformed officers, forensics professionals, and detectives through in the two months since the incident. I saw evidence of their presence at every turn, though it irritated me far less than it would have in a case where the evidence was fresher. I quickly turned my attention to the structure of the house and how it lay within the yard and the surrounding residences.

I had seen photos from the time of the incident, so I knew that Lewis normally kept a well-maintained lawn. His lot was of average size, with homes on the left and right. The 911 neighbor lived to the left. To the right, the family had been on vacation at the time. The backyard had a high fence with a gate. I walked toward it, flashlight shining, and noticed that the opening was on Lewis's side, though the latch was loose and could be easily manipulated from the other side as well. It was a privacy fence, rather than a security measure.

After walking the yard, I went back through the house. I hadn't expected to find mountains of fresh evidence, but I had hoped I might find something more conclusive, that magic spark that would break the case open. But that happens far more rarely in life than it does in mystery novels, and Lester's officers were at least competent enough in their jobs not to miss the utterly obvious.

I left, feeling neither frustrated nor elated. I had done my due diligence, but I needed input from elsewhere to tell me if anything I had seen meant anything in particular.

I spent most of the night preparing the zoning transcript. The dullest jobs always order expedited delivery. I didn't mind the lack of sleep, though Johnny found time to lecture me about my unhealthy habits over his morning coffee. He might as well have lectured the dead. My mind was fixed on my certainty that Lewis was innocent and the lack of signposts helping to point the way to how it could be possible. I set off to interview the neighbor from directly across the street, who had been home on the night of the incident, hoping to elicit something the police had missed.

The Happy Hare was a British-themed diner that was draped with nearly as many Union Flags as grease stains. I had been there exactly once before, though, if you have read Johnny's stories (as I am told many now have), you would know that it was an important one time, for it was there, at the sticky corner booth, that Johnny and I were introduced to one another as potential roommates. I had seen his laugh lines and threadbare dress shirt and the careful way he kept the photos of his nieces and nephews as if they were worth millions. He had let his intuition guide him regarding me, and we had decided to move in together, a defense attorney and a court reporter. I'm not sentimental, but I let the memory gambol across my mind for a moment before I snapped myself back to the present reality.

Kitty Williamson was working, as I'd been promised she would be over the phone, but I arrived after the breakfast rush, and only one table was occupied. I was shown to a small, round table by the young hostess, and then the server emerged from the kitchen. She was wearing the diner's uniform of plaid trousers and white shirt. "Miss Williamson?" I said. "I'd like to ask you about the case involving Charles Lewis. I'm working with his attorney." I didn't see a need to maintain my usual built-in cover of court reporting. If she'd pressed for a name, I would have given an alias, but beyond that, I hoped the encounter would be straightforward.

"Me?" She looked surprised as she stood in front me. "The police already talked to me, and I don't know anything."

"I have more questions," I said, "if you don't mind, of course."

"Well, okay," she answered, a bit hesitantly. "I can take my break and let Lee-Ann take over."

She sat across from me a few moments later, both of us armed with mugs of tea. "I really have one main question," I said, seeing no reason to dissemble or waste time. "Did anything, anything at all, happen on Briar Street the night Lewis was arrested? I know an event like that tends to take all the attention and make anything else seem insignificant. But please, if you remember anything, even if it seems unimportant or normal, tell me."

She thought for a few moments. "I worked the breakfast-lunch shift and came home. There wasn't anything strange. Like everyone said, I didn't hear anyone, and there weren't strange cars on the street or anything. It's pretty quiet. I mean, we hear sirens a lot because the hospital is so close. That's about all."

She continued. "The only thing that happened was poor Mrs. Gray getting an ambulance again. She's not on my street. She's one over, right behind Lewis's house. We all thought it was too bad because out of everyone, she might have heard something if she'd been there when it happened."

This checked out with what I had read in the police report from Johnny, that Mrs. Gray, from the brick house behind Lewis's, hadn't been interviewed because she was in the hospital. *In the hospital.*

Something jogged in my mind, and I felt the hairs on the back of my neck start to prickle. Kitty had no idea what a potential bomb she'd dropped on me, and I intended to keep it that way. I forced myself to ask her five or six other inconsequential questions and feigned interest. But my mind was racing elsewhere.

As soon as I could get away, I went back to my car, blood pumping in my ears. I took my case file off the passenger's seat and leafed through it, frustrated at the time it took me to locate the police summary packet Johnny had given me.

Did not interview Sylvia Gray, neighboring homeowner. According to doctor, hospitalized with complications of cardiac illness since May 11th. No one else in the home.

May 11th. Three days before the day Charles Lewis had come home to find a body in the front hallway of his house. And three days before an ambulance had come to her house to take her away—to the hospital where she was already lying in bed in the cardiac ward.

I needed confirmation.

Lewis's 911 neighbor was a Mrs. Barnett, who lived with her husband and two cats. She answered the phone as soon as I called, and, as the one who had achieved a small amount of notoriety for her role in the case, was more than eager to discuss it with anyone who asked, regardless of how much the State frowned on it.

"Oh, yes," she said, "Mrs. Gray from the big brick house had an ambulance come just before it all happened. They didn't use sirens or anything, just came to get her like usual. We're so close to the hospital, you know. Sometimes she goes in and out of the hospital two or three times in one week; they'll take her money any time, you know. She keeps to herself, and none of us really know her that well. I feel bad saying negative things about a sick person, but she's just there with her house and her Cadillac. Drives herself sometimes, too, if she doesn't want the ambulance for some reason. Won't take help from anyone. Kind of erratic, if you ask me. I couldn't tell you when she was in or out of the neighborhood over the past year if I tried."

"Did you mention this to the police?" I asked.

"No," she answered. "I mean, they probably found out, since they went around to all the neighbors. But Mrs. Gray gets an ambulance all the time. She has heart problems, and she's really old and has a lot of money. I'm sure nobody even gave it a second thought because it happens all the time. She's convinced she's going to die, but she never does."

I hung up and thought of a morgue attendant named Jeremy Stills, a morgue attendant who had reported a body missing on the night of May 14th and been told by his superiors that nothing was wrong, that his Jane Doe had never even existed.

I looked back at my interview notes, at the story the nervous young man had repeated several times, scared we would dismiss him like everyone else had.

"She bled out, stab wounds. The body barely made it down to me before I took my break, and then she was—gone. They do the police reports upstairs, from the emergency room exam. But there weren't any suspects or anything because someone just found her on the street and brought her in, just before she went. I was going to find out what happened because I was curious, but—she wasn't there anymore."

It couldn't be. It was too preposterous.

But, just a few blocks away from Midtown General, was a neighborhood with a brick house and a gate that didn't lock, where an ambulance had come to pick up a woman who wasn't even there.

You were right. Johnny

I'm sure I was, but please elaborate. S.

Johnny's text message arrested my pondering.

I called Lewis and pushed him about the ring. Told him it could be life or death. He admits had an eight-year relationship with the senior staff doctor of Midtown General. Ended because he had an affair four months ago. Swears he didn't think it was relevant.

I laughed aloud, sitting alone in the apartment. "Didn't think it was relevant."

"Why was an ambulance at the house of Mrs. Gray if she was already in the hospital?" Johnny blinked in confusion, sitting across the living room from me with a judgmental scowl because I was vaping, which he despised.

"To transport Jane Doe's body and deposit it in the vestibule of your client," I answered. "That's how Lewis's enraged medical ex must have managed it. She surely had help. I don't even know if she went herself, though I suspect she did, to make sure the body stayed in the right condition."

My friend shook his head and exhaled sharply. "I can't believe it. It's too insane."

"Corpses are a very difficult thing to misplace in this day and time. The plot is unraveling, and the morgue attendant can't be the only one who noticed something odd, surely. You know the final autopsy revealed time of death and cause discrepancies, just nothing conclusive enough to get Lewis off. It should have happened sooner, if the police had learned about the ambulance and questioned it, but of course they didn't."

Johnny was staring at me. "I swear you're beyond human," he said. "How can you assimilate this theory so calmly?"

"As you know, my method is to answer questions using observable facts. My first question, about your client's innocence, I answered to my satisfaction. That settled, I knew there must be an answer to how the corpse was foisted on him, however weird it might turn out to be, and, since a more commonplace solution was not forthcoming, I had begun to suspect something more. What we need is a link between the hospital and Laura Anderson, some other evidence of a Jane Doe being processed through the system before disappearing. I'll call in a favor and get Lester on it."

I preferred to do my own legwork, but it was far easier for Lester to get official people to give official access. As soon as I told him my needs pertained to his missing body case, he was eager to get me what I needed.

That's why, the following morning, I received a phone call from him instead of a text, which irritated me. "Sharon, I've got what you asked for!" His tone was absolutely elated. "They went into the system records, and, sure enough, on the night of May 14th, the ER admitted a Jane Doe with stab wounds. Originally, an order was put in to call the police, and an entire file, including time of death, was recorded. But then—it vanished. The IT guy who looked it up for me said it was so weird he thought it might be a system malfunction. The entire patient record was deleted using the login of a Nurse named Lucy Carter. He was only able to call it up using the system backup."

I had listened silently up to this point, minding less by the second that he had called instead of texting. "We'll have to follow up with that nurse."

Lester's voice took on an even more self-satisfied tone. "I knew you'd think I wouldn't have done it, but I did. She's the nurse who works directly with the chief of the medical staff, and she's already admitted to deleting the patient file, though she swears she has no idea why her boss told her to do it."

I was tempted to compliment Lester, but I have my limits. "Very good," I said, as a general comment on the situation. "Do you want me to tell you what I know?"

"Diabolical," said my friend, who wasn't normally dramatic. I'd met him for lunch at the sandwich bar across the street from the courthouse.

"Agreed," I said, "but, as with most would-be master criminals, the doctor is not nearly as smart as she thinks she is. She waited for the perfect corpse, but it's too difficult to get rid of someone without a trace these days."

"Framing someone for murder isn't the most aggressive thing I've seen someone do out of a jealous desire for revenge," Johnny mused, "But it's one of the most ingenious."

I continued my explanation. "She knew the neighborhood routines from living there briefly at the end of the relationship, and her biggest risk was in the situation with Mrs. Gray, but she correctly judged that the neighbors wouldn't be sure about the going and coming of the private old lady, at least not enough to question the normalcy of an ambulance coming to the house. Besides, if anyone had noticed at the time, I'm sure she had a story waiting. But she didn't need it. No one questioned the obvious signs of Lewis's guilt enough to pursue other avenues of inquiry, and certainly no one connected a random Jane Doe from the hospital with your case, especially once the police had discovered the victim was Laura Anderson."

"Except us," said Johnny, raising his coffee mug.

"Except us," I echoed, clinking mugs and indulging his partnership toast, not really minding at all.

"Lester says Lewis can't be released yet," he added after a moment. "He believes us, but he can't force the State."

"Yes," I sighed. "This is incredibly difficult to prove, two months after the fact. Any physical evidence at the house has been destroyed, and even if the loss of a Jane Doe is proven on the hospital side, there's no record that it was Laura Anderson. I've promised Lester I'll keep trying. But, Johnny, if you do go to trial, you can introduce reasonable doubt, especially since no one, even before this, had ever managed to connect Lewis with Anderson. At least we have an alternate, possible theory to present to the jury, and the neighbors will have to testify that Lewis and the doctor were in a relationship." It wasn't a clear-cut victory, not yet.

Lester was bringing the doctor in for questioning by himself and other officers. I could not be present, since practically the entire division was aware and involved because of her prominent position. She was the unseen player in the whole thing, whose presence I somehow felt breathing down the back of my neck as I thought about it. Lester's hope was that confronting her, on top of her nurse caving to police pressure and agreeing to testify to the deletion of patient records, would lead her to some kind of admission.

I was not so sure.

Dr. Jessica, the remarkable scorned lover of the unremarkable Charles Lewis, was released from police custody within one day. "Insufficient evidence. No formal charges. Crazy theories by the police that the State couldn't validate." All of these buzzed across the TV and online news, as pictures of an earnest-looking, middle-aged doctor in scrubs helped reduce the case to nothing but another instance of absurd harassment against an innocent woman by overzealous law enforcement.

I was taking a deposition when the news dropped. By the time I got home to the apartment, I found a letter shoved underneath the door. A real, handwritten letter. Neat and analogue and as infuriating as the sight of the red ink against the bright white paper background.

You're It, Helms.

Love,
Dr. Jessica March

ABOUT THE CONTRIBUTORS

Phil Attwell is a Sherlockian who co-wrote "The Oxford of Inspector Morse" and has penned the odd article over the years.

Chris Aarnes Bakkane says "I'm a trans, Norwegian hopeless romantic born in 1992 that has a passionate interest in the adventures of Sherlock Holmes and his intimate friend and partner Doctor John H. Watson. I'd always been interested in the Holmes stories, but it wasn't until 2015 during my bachelor's degree in film – when I rediscovered the Granada series starring Jeremy Brett, David Burke and Edward Hardwicke respectively – that I fully fell in love with the characters and started to reintroduce myself into the Canon. Now, graduated with a master's degree in film and a little older, I've gotten more invested in the various adaptations mostly in film and TV (being my field of study), but also in radio, literature and comic books. I also started doing freelance illustrative work and commissions related to Conan Doyle's characters, specifically Holmes and Watson. This is work I really enjoy, and my wish would be able to create more art and write stories relating to the characters. My hope would then be to be able to share my art and stories with other Sherlockians around the world, but also try to contribute to the ever-growing pool of Sherlockian content in both art, literature and other fields of study."

Mary-Catherine Berger is a University Freshman studying Chemistry and English. She has been in Sherlock fandom for just over two years but has been a fan of the detective and his stories since she was 9. She is staff member Cumbercookie on the Three Patch Podcast and can be found in various fandom spaces including AO3 as HPswl_cumbercookie.

Mattias Boström is the author of Agatha Award winning From Holmes to Sherlock: The Story of the Men and Women Who Created an Icon (Mysterious Press, 2017), which won several other prizes and was nominated for Edgar, Anthony, and Macavity awards. He writes occasionally for the Baker Street Journal and is main editor of the Sherlock Holmes and Conan Doyle in the Newspapers series (Gasogene Books). He lives outside Stockholm with his wife and two daughters, is a member of the Baker Street Irregulars, an honorary member of the Baskerville Hall Club of Sweden, and also a member of several other Sherlockian societies around the world.

Merinda Brayfield is a writer by day, IT wizard by night living in Texas. She has a self-published book and written over 500 unique stories to date. Merinda has recently featured in The Watsonian with her piece "That Day" and the Spark newsletter. Merinda is a semi-professional extrovert who spends her time immersed in Twitter as @merindab, fangirling about Doctor Who and cuddling her dog, Church.

Margie Deck (Spanaway, WA, USA) lives in the Pacific Northwest with a pile of books, a husband, and a dog. When not wiling away her time talking about Sherlock Holmes on Twitter (@pawkypuzzler), she stays busy playing the game with The Sound of the Baskervilles, The Dogs in the Nighttime, The John H Watson Society, the Left Coast Sherlockian Symposium, and The Stormy Petrels of BC.

Wanda Dow is a retired Data Technician who lives in New Mexico. She is a founding member of The Pleasant Places of Florida, a Sherlockian Scion. She is also the author of the Phoenix and Chen book series (under the pseudonym Wanda Iola). **Jeff Dow** is a retired City/Transportation Planner who lives in New Mexico. He is the webmaster of The Pleasant Places of Florida, a Sherlockian Scion. He is also the author of the Dragon's Eye Moon book series. Together with their children, they are The Dow Family Players and have performed many Holmesian skits at club functions throughout the years.

Morton L Duffy writes fun, traditional and urban fantasy, action-packed mysteries featuring clever, brave characters with endearing flaws. Free reads can be found at https://www.indipenned.com/index.php?p1=6waystosunday&p2 =blog and Morton is on Twitter @Morton100.

Trudence Holtz, first of her name. Her goals vary between sleeping a lot and learning to read faster. Can often be found insisting she can finish one more chapter before bedtime. Trudy was the first official member of Doyle's Rotary Coffin, despite not asking to be.

iamjohnlocked4life (JL4L): Known in fandom spaces as Johnlocked or JL, iamjohnlocked4life has been part of the Sherlock Holmes online fandom since 2014. She makes fanart and writes fanfic on Archive of Our Own, and is part of the main staff on the Three Patch Podcast. A lifelong congoer and cosplayer, JL can usually be found in costume at 221B Con in Atlanta. She loves podcasts, podfics, and Pokémon Go, and is a devoted champion for unconventional Sherlock Holmes adaptations, especially those with female leads.

Roger Johnson is a retired librarian, currently working as a volunteer guide at Essex Police Museum. In his spare time he edits The Sherlock Holmes Journal for the Sherlock Holmes Society of London, and contributes forewords to other people's books. He and his wife Jean Upton, a fellow-Holmesian, live in a small Edwardian house between Chelmsford Prison and Essex Police Headquarters, with three cats and several thousand books.

Brad Keefauver writes, podcasts and emits Sherlock Holmes as much as possible, going back to the late 1970s, having imprinted upon the great detective at age thirteen upon seeing *The Private Life of Sherlock Holmes* movie trailer at a theater called "The Strand." The movie *Holmes and Watson* raised his Sherlockian consciousness to new levels and helped him find inner peace, acceptance of all Sherlocks, and at least one comedic bit that he commits to much too hard. He blogs as "Sherlock Peoria" and hosts "The Watsonian Weekly" podcast.

Bob Madia has been writing since he was young and has been a Sherlockian since he was 10. He is the Sherlock Expert for WGN Radio host Nick DiGilio in Chicago and is a professional screenwriter. He has two features (Closets and You Can't Kill Stephen King) available on DVD and streaming services. He is married with one daughter (Sarah, not Anna).

Paul Thomas Miller should be ashamed of himself. He is the current chairman of The Shingle of Southsea and a member of several other Holmesian organisations. He recently published his first book, a Holmesian chronology called Watson Does Not Lie.

Les Moskowitz from the U.S. is a New York transplant currently living in Florida, by way of Maryland. His Sherlockian career dates back to 1968, when he attended his first meeting of The Six Napoleons of Baltimore, and has been a member of various Sherlockian societies since that time. He is a past list owner of the "Hounds of the Internet" mailing list and is the author of "Canonical Variations", a study which compares the text of the original Strand version of the Canon with the Doubleday edition.

Robert Perret wrote a long running but poorly circulated comic strip in middle school entitled Wipeout Willy. In college he published the embarrassingly pretentious Wafflehaus in the campus paper. In the following couple of decades he had rendered the occasional rude doodle. He is a member of JHWS, SOB, and Doyle's Rotary Coffin.

#PoetOnaBike is autistic and is on Twitter occasionally.

Shai Porter says of herself: Hello. My name is Shai. I like to write things about Sherlock Holmes. I have two cats. They eat paper and plastic. Thank you for reading my story.

Spacefall tends books for a living and spends their free time drawing cyborgs.

Vince Stadon writes lots of silly things for various silly publications. He lives in Bristol, UK, with cats of undetermined loyalty and a wife with exacting standards of pedantry.

Thinkanddoodle is a fandom-renowned artist from Belgium. Her work is recognized and admired by fans all over the globe. As an art teacher by day and beloved fanartist by night, she does her best to inspire and motivate others with her talents and skills. Her most-used mediums and programs include Photoshop and Krita, but occasionally she loves to slip back to her roots using sketchbooks and fine liners. You can follow Thinkanddoodle on Twitter (@thinkanddoodle), Tumblr (thinkanddoodle-batch), Instagram (thinkanddoodle_batch), as well as order products and prints through her store at Thinkanddoodle.redbubble.com

Amy Thomas is a freelance writer and editor who podcasts with the Baker Street Babes. She is the author of The Detective and The Woman novels featuring Sherlock Holmes and Irene Adler. No Holmesian adaptation is too outlandish, too silly, or too unusual for her to review and enjoy.

Toti was born in Bogotá-Colombia where she studies acting and writes as a hobby. Thanks to BBC Sherlock she got started writing poetry. She can be found on Twitter as @poeticholmes.

Samuel Verner is a member of the Sound of the Baskervilles, John H. Watson Society, and Doyle's Rotary Coffin.

Margaret Walsh was born and raised in the antipodes, and is the author of "Sherlock Holmes and the Molly-Boy Murders" published by MX Publishing. A devotee of Sherlock Holmes since childhood. Has an ongoing love affair with the city of London. She is a member of Doyle's Rotary Coffin. You can find her tweeting away on Twitter at @EspineuxAlpha.

DOYLE'S ROTARY COFFIN

Doyle's Rotary Coffin is a society formed for the sole purpose of whole-heartedly and contrarily enjoying stupid Holmesiana regardless of how Canonical others consider it to be. The society was originally formed shortly after the release of Holmes and Watson (the 2018 Will Ferrell and John C. Reilly film) as a counter-reaction to the negativity the film attracted from the Holmesian community. Originally it was about enjoying the stupidest parts of Holmesiana as the best parts of Holmesiana regardless of evidence or opinion to the contrary. But it soon went a bit deeper. We wanted to argue that there is something positive to say about every iteration of Holmes. And we wanted to affirm that the more Holmes's you find something positive in, the more enjoyment you will get out of Holmesiana. In this way, we are very much joining a tradition already created by the Baker Street Babes with their battle cry: "All Holmes is Good Holmes".

It became clear that the championing of inclusivity and positivity in Holmesiana was something a lot of us felt was important and wanted to make a conscious effort to be better at ourselves and this quickly became a part of our ethos. Hence the society motto:

No Holmes Barred
Especially Dreadful Holmes, Bizarre Holmes and Sacrilegious Holmes.

Now this is a central tenant of Doyle's Rotary Coffin. Originally our thinking was limited to dramatic portrayal. But it is clear it applies to pastiche, parody, interpretations, theories, societies, events, jokes, art... and any other way of adapting or using Holmes you can imagine. So, why such positivity for all Holmes, often in defiance of rational thought? There are many reasons, often overlapping, and I'd like to try to explain a few here:

1. The more Holmes exists, the more there is to enjoy. You might not necessarily directly enjoy a Holmes, but whatever it brings to the table gives you something to have fun looking at with other Holmesians. Something to talk about. Something to direct your shared passion towards.

2. The more Holmes you enjoy, the happier you'll be. If you make a slight effort to find enjoyment in more Holmeses, you've just expanded the playing field for your own Holmesiana.

3. More Holmes means more Holmesians. While you might be unable to find anything to love about a Holmes, every single Holmes stands a chance of bringing more people to the Holmesian party. And the Holmesian party is always improved by more people. More people means more ideas. Which means more creativity. Which means more creation. Which means more to enjoy, whether that is content, conversations or just plain shenanigans.

4. Being positive about anything breeds positivity. Both for you and for those around you. Negativity - not so much. Start trying to enjoy more Holmesiana - even the stupid stuff, and you'll pretty soon discover you are having a better Holmesian time. Honest. I'm talking from experience here.

5. Perhaps, most importantly, if there is a Holmes you find you can't enjoy, be grateful it exists anyway. Don't just tolerate it, you should be actively pleased it exists. Trust me, there are Holmesian things I can't be doing with. Let's call them "X". I've tried to find my joy in "X", and failed. But there's a million other Holmeses for me to go look at instead. So rather than ruin "X" for others, I go look at the stuff I do like. Not only that, I am truly grateful that "X" exists, because it is bringing more people to Holmes which means more fun for all Holmesians.

With all enthusiasm, then, I can happily declare:

No Holmes Barred
Especially Dreadful Holmes, Bizarre Holmes and Sacrilegious Holmes.

For more information about Doyle's Rotary Coffin, to read more or to print yourself a membership card, please visit

doylesrotarycoffin.com

To make any suggestions or to send contributions to the site please contact

DoylesRotaryCoffin@outlook.com

Printed in Great Britain
by Amazon